CRIME LORD'S
PARADISE

CRIME LORD SERIES, BOOK 4.5

MIA KNIGHT

COPYRIGHT

DEDICATION

To those who can't get enough of Gavin Pyre. This is for you.

1

THE SOUND OF HER FEET RHYTHMICALLY HITTING THE treadmill was the only sound in the exercise room. Listening to music only distracted her from what she was doing. Her eyes moved restlessly over the mirrored walls to reassure her that she was alone. The machine's display was covered by a gun and her cell phone. The phone played a live video feed of Nora asleep in the nursery.

Lyla embraced the burn. Running had become her go-to when she couldn't sleep or when her stress level was through the roof. She trained with Blade daily even though Gavin was out of the underworld. It kept her active, focused, and ready for anything.

It had been three months since Steven Vega died in Hell. Three months yet it felt like yesterday. Some days she felt normal, hopeful even. Other days, she felt as if she had weights strapped to her ankles. Today was one of those days. She wanted to lock herself in the basement, turn off the lights, and deal with her demons in peace.

As if on cue, the door behind her opened, and a man in a suit entered. She watched him approach in the mirror. Her husband stopped beside the treadmill. She got a whiff of his cologne as she panted, and he smelled amazing, as usual. He was home later than normal. She'd been grateful for the reprieve, so she could work out her bad mood because she wasn't up for an interrogation. There was no doubt in her mind that's what she was in for after her excursion today. Blade never failed to fill Gavin in on every little thing.

"You're done," Gavin said.

"I just started," she puffed. "Give me thirty minutes. I'll meet you upstairs."

He slapped the off button, and the tread immediately slowed from a sprint to a walk. She glared at him. He looked as alert as he'd been when he left at four this morning. His gray tailored suit fit his broad, muscled frame perfectly. His white shirt was open at the throat, showing off his tanned, defined chest. Black hair was slicked back, and his stunning amber eyes were assessing as they moved over her. She wanted to bite him for looking so composed and controlled. Nothing affected him.

She hopped off the machine and paced with her hands on her hips. "I left some food out for you."

He didn't reply. A quick glance in the mirror confirmed he was tracking her as she circled away from him. She didn't want to be touched right now. She wanted to be alone, but clearly, he wasn't going to accommodate what she wanted. She didn't want to discuss it. Gavin could be bullheaded when it came to ripping off Band-Aids, and she wasn't ready.

"I'll meet you in the kitchen," she said pointedly, willing him to leave her be.

"Come here."

She shook her head as she marched restlessly. "Give me ten minutes."

All day she kept a chokehold on her emotions for Nora's sake. She did her mommy role the best she could when she wanted to shoot something. Now that her baby was asleep, it was her time. Or it would have been if Gavin would give her space.

"I just need some time alone, Gavin."

"You're not gonna get it."

She whipped her head around. "I don't interfere with your workout time!"

He walked to the punching bag and reached for something. When he turned, she saw he was holding black hand wraps.

"Blade says you like boxing. We can do some mitt training," he said.

Blade introduced her to boxing two months ago, and it had quickly become her latest obsession. It would take hours of running to take the edge off her foul mood, but boxing would accomplish the release she needed in half the time. She came forward and held out her hand for him to bind it. He grasped it and drew her against him.

"Kiss me."

She looked up. Intense hazel eyes bored into her. His energy pulsed in the air. Gavin was always on, always ready for anything. In the past, she shied away from his aggression, but now, she leaned into it. He was her savage. He may spend most of his days in an office tapping at a keyboard, but her husband was a warrior beneath the ten thousand-dollar suits. They had been through hell and back together.

She braced a hand on his muscled chest and rose to her tiptoes. She gave him a quick, close mouthed kiss. When she would have pulled away, he grasped her nape to keep her close and applied pressure on her chin so her mouth opened. He covered her lips with his and slanted his head to go deep. His tongue stroked hers, and he let out a low growl of pleasure. He drank from her as if he couldn't get enough. She dug her nails into his chest and tensed, fighting his drugging effect on her. He massaged her neck, coaxing her to relax, but she couldn't. She was too revved up. She pushed away from him and staggered back.

Gavin's hand hovered between them for a few beats before he dropped it. A muscle flexed in his cheek. She roused the lion. She could see it watching her. Baiting him was never wise, but she didn't want to be soothed or petted. She wanted to fight. Today had been an emotional roller coaster, and sex wasn't going to cut it.

"Not now," she said.

Gavin held out his hand again. She hesitated before she extended hers. He slipped off her wedding ring and pocketed it before he began to wrap her hands. "You want to fight first? Fine with me."

"You're the one who suggested boxing," she said.

He taped her hands swiftly, with the ease of someone who did this often.

"When you're pissed off, nothing's better than stepping into the ring," he said.

"You still train while you're at work?" she asked.

"Every day."

That explained his even temper and ridiculous body. She trained in mixed martial arts, boxing, guns, and anything else Blade decided to throw at her. She had lost a lot of the baby weight she gained during her pregnancy, but she was nowhere close to having a six-pack.

As she put on her gloves, Gavin shrugged off his jacket and shirt. The light bounced off the fresh scar on his back that he received from a whip. Her hands fisted in the gloves. Fucking Steven. If she could kill him again, she would. She witnessed his death and even kicked his head after it was severed from his body, but it wasn't enough. Nothing would be. He had been gone for months, but the rage and pain still festered inside her. Steven forced her to change into a different person, and there was no going back to what she had been before he ripped their world apart. On days like this, when she felt as if she would explode, she longed for a place to let loose the way she had in the pit of Hell. That barbaric place allowed her to indulge in baser instincts she didn't know she possessed.

Gavin walked toward her. She admired the ripple of muscles and took note of the bare feet peeking out from his slacks. She raised her gloves and got into her stance. His eyes warmed with approval as he raised his punching mitts.

"Let's do this."

He started her off with some basic boxing combinations. The sound of her glove making contact with his mitt was immensely satisfying.

"Harder," he said, and she complied with relish.

Gavin kept her on her toes. His brand of training was more aggressive than Blade's. His technique and fancy footwork told her she was in the ring with a master, as if she didn't already know that. He handled swords with the same ease that he did guns. There was a lot to learn from her husband.

She didn't have the headspace to think about anything but survival. Sweat poured down her back, and her arms ached, but she didn't stop. She focused on landing accurate hits, being light on her feet, and not getting cornered. Every move he made, she countered. He called out the combinations, and she obeyed. Jab, cross, uppercut, cross.

He advanced, which forced her to retreat and then fight to regain ground. He called out a series of combinations, which caused her to duck and slip. He jabbed. Her reflexes saved her from a tap that would have knocked her on her ass. She knew she was in no danger since he was pulling his punches, but the near miss made her heart race. Gavin was built like a tank, and the largest opponent she had ever faced off with. He was pushing her to react instinctively. She struck out with a left hook that grazed his chin. He stepped back and stared at her for a long moment before he stripped off the mitts and then unbuckled his belt.

"Gavin!"

"What?"

He tossed the belt and unbuttoned his slacks. He didn't pull down the zipper, but he didn't need to. He was stating his intentions as if his erection wasn't obvious enough. Her body responded even though she didn't want it to. It was hard not to ogle him when his body glistened with sweat. They were playing a mental and physical game that was stimulating in more ways than one.

He held up his palms. "Come here."

She hesitated, eyes dipping to his bulge before she came within striking distance. When he gave her a new combination, she eased back into the exercise, tapping her gloves to his bare hands. She lost herself in the repetition and moved with him. She wasn't prepared when he grabbed her oversized shirt and yanked her against him. His mouth landed on hers at the same time as he gripped her hair to keep her in place.

She wrenched their lips apart and winced when he tugged off her rubber band. Her hair cascaded around her. "Stop!"

"You think I can watch you fight and not fuck you?"

A solid left hook caught him on the ear and allowed her

to dance backward. Her body tingled as he surveyed her with the eyes of a predator.

"You want to play dirty, baby girl?"

His voice caused goose bumps to erupt over her body. She'd gone too far, but that had never stopped her before.

"No, I don't want to play dirty. I want to box," she panted.

"No, you want to fight," he corrected.

His stillness made her heart race. She took two more steps back even though distance wouldn't make a difference. Her husband was a master of war. She'd seen him in action. She had no chance of escaping him, but that didn't mean she wouldn't try.

"Lucky for you, I'm willing to oblige," he said gently.

The sound of his zipper being undone seemed unnaturally loud. She looked around, but there was nowhere to run. She backed onto some padded floor mats and Gavin followed, clad in only black boxers.

"Gavin, let me run on the treadmill for a half hour," she said raggedly.

Her arms trembled from boxing, but her chest was still tight with emotion. She was hyped on adrenaline and close to burning herself out. If they trained a little longer, she might get a decent night of sleep.

"You're overworking your body."

"I'm fine!"

"You trained two hours this morning, and now you're going at it again," he said, revealing exactly how familiar he was with her daily activities. "You're done."

"I'm not! I need a little more—"

She didn't get a chance to finish her sentence because he lunged. He dodged her jab and kicked her legs out from under her. She landed flat on her back with the wind knocked out of her. When he crouched over her, she boxed his head, enraged at his foul play.

"You cheated!" she shouted.

"When have I ever played fair?"

He stripped off her gloves and kissed her taped, sweaty fists.

"We are *not* having sex!"

His grin made her see red. She positioned her feet on his hips and propelled herself away from him. He cursed as she leapt to her feet, but before she could take a step, a stinging grip on her ankle yanked her off balance. Her hands hit the ground to break her fall and then scrabbled over the mat as he yanked her backward with a grip on her shirt, ripping the thin material over her shoulders. In full combat mode, she kicked back with her free leg and caught him on the chest. He growled as he flipped her on her back.

"You want to fight, baby?"

"No!" she spat as he yanked her ruined shirt from her body. "I want to be left alone!"

"How many times have you asked me to let you go and how many times have I done it? Never." His hand closed around her throat and squeezed. "The more you fight, the more I want you. You should know that by now." She went still beneath him, and he smiled. "Playing possum isn't going to work."

He tucked his face against her neck. His deep inhale made her pussy clench.

"I want you more now than I did when you were young and worshipped me."

"Those days are long gone," she snapped.

She grabbed his thumb and yanked savagely, loosening his hold on her neck. She would have squirmed out from under him, but his weight kept her in place.

"Yes, they are," he agreed and pinned her hands over her head and unzipped her sports bra. "Now I don't need to hold back." He squeezed her nipple and grinned at her enraged bellow. "Still sensitive, baby?"

"Yes, you fuck! I told you not to—" Her voice died when he put his mouth on her breast. She bucked beneath him, but he didn't move an inch. Fucking tank. "Gavin, don't!"

He mumbled something around her nipple and sucked hard enough to make her curse.

"I'm going to kill you!" she shouted.

"Then who's gonna take care of Nora in the middle of the night?" he asked absently as he massaged her breast. "What's this bruise?"

"Nora! Apparently, she likes to bite just like you, you ass!"

He chuckled. "That's my girl. She's getting wilder by the day."

"Yes, and you're not helping. You give her everything she wants."

"Of course, I do. Just as I give you what you need."

"You're *not* giving me what I need! I told you I want to be alone."

He flicked her nipple with his tongue. She jerked as a streak of lightning shot through her.

"What you want and what you need aren't the same thing. Lucky for you, I know the difference."

"I told you I'm not in the mood." She shrieked when he bit her. "Cut it out!"

"Don't lie," he said, laving her tortured nipple with his tongue. "You want me."

"I'm not lying. I don't want ..." Her voice died when he cupped her.

"What's this?" he asked silkily.

"That's sweat."

"Don't fuck with me, Lyla."

"Give me twenty minutes."

Gavin trained her from a young age to respond to him, and unfortunately, she'd never become desensitized. No matter what he did, she wanted him. But she didn't want him when her head was fucked up and her blood was boiling.

"Twenty minutes for what? To beat the punching bag until you're exhausted? As it is, you're going to be sore tomorrow. You won't be able to hold Nora."

"You don't know that."

"I do," he said with such confidence that she believed him. "There are other ways to work out your demons, baby girl." His fingers worked between her legs, wedging the thin material of her yoga pants in places it shouldn't be and began to rub expertly.

She grabbed his wrist but didn't possess the strength to pull his hand away. In the end, she was helping him. They stared at one another as she soaked her underwear.

"Blade's training is showing," he said gruffly as his eyes moved over her topless body. "You're not allowed to train with anyone but him. I don't want anyone seeing you like this."

"Like what?"

"Angry, slick, fierce. That's mine." He licked her chest scars and hummed as if he was tasting a delicacy. "We should spar more often."

She panted as the heat between them built. He was channeling her dark emotions into something else. He applied more pressure, which made her thighs tremble. His eyes were lighter now, revealing that his beast was completely aroused. She rocked her hips into his hand and stilled as a memory began to intrude, snuffing out desire and replacing it with icy rage.

"Let me—" she tried to negotiate.

He pressed his forehead against hers. "Focus."

She glared at him. "You fucking focus."

One hand cupped her face while the other continued to stroke her. "Stay with me."

"I'm right here."

"No, you're somewhere you don't need to be."

Her chest ached with feelings she couldn't set free. She closed her eyes as he pressed light kisses over her face.

"Feel me, Lyla." His lips slid to her cheek and then her neck. "I need you here with me."

Her breath hitched as he sucked on her neck.

"I can't fix it if you don't tell me."

"There's no fixing this." A cloud of hopelessness had hovered over her all day, and she combatted this by being pissed off. It was better than crying.

"No matter what, we have each other," he rumbled.

The invisible pressure on her chest lightened. He was right. Even if the world went to shit outside their fortress, they still had one another. They should have died in Hell. By some miracle, they made it out with the whiplash on his back and some filthy memories she would never be able to purge. It was a small price to pay.

She slid her fingers into his hair and destroyed his slick do. She tugged on his hair, forcing his lips from her neck so she could move them to hers. This time, it was her tongue that intruded. She was the aggressor for the two seconds it took for him to participate. When his thumb rubbed her nub, she groaned and arched against him. She felt his lips curve against hers and broke the kiss.

"You with me?" he murmured with a wicked grin.

"Let me up," she ordered.

He hesitated before he rolled to the side. When she rose, he grabbed her calf to stop her from moving away, but his grip relaxed when she pushed her pants down. He helped her pull them off before he kissed her lower stomach and then nuzzled her pussy. His hands kneaded her ass before gliding down the back of her legs. The erotic sight of her massive husband kneeling before her as he ate her out made her body flush with heat.

"Gavin," she whispered.

He draped her leg over one shoulder for better access. She tipped her head back and clenched her teeth as he teased her. When it was too much for her, she jerked away and clamped her quaking thighs together. He wiped his face as got to his feet, clutching his cock.

"Your choice," he rumbled.

She glanced around and pointed at the adjustable bench seat, which had the back up. When he sat, she straddled him. He immediately pressed his cock to her opening and penetrated. He buried his face against her breasts and let out a jagged breath as she settled on his lap.

She looped her arms around his neck. "You feel good."

His hands flexed on her. "You talk like that; this slow shit ends."

"We wouldn't want that. We just started."

She rolled her hips. He was letting her set the pace, which was a rare occurrence. He was giving her back a measure of control when she needed it. Her hands glided over his muscles, which shifted beneath her palms. His low growl of encouragement made her smile. She nuzzled him as she rolled her hips. His lips sampled her shoulder, the curve of her breast, and the line of her throat. He was loving her out of her melancholy, something he had been doing often in the past few weeks.

"I like being on top." Her feet were touching the ground, which allowed her to control her rise and fall. "You like this, baby?"

The cords in his neck bulged as he held himself in check. When she rose, he bucked as he tried to keep himself inside her. His hands went to her hips to keep her in place.

She raised a brow. "Not fast enough?"

He flexed his hands before he loosened his hold. Starving eyes laced with lust made her body tingle.

"Do what you want before I take over," he said in a guttural tone.

She leaned back, braced her hands on his thick thighs, and bucked her hips up to take him. Her stomach muscles burned as she rocked. Gavin gripped her waist, gaze fixated on his dick sinking into her body. She let her head fall back, closed her eyes, and took what she wanted. Gavin applied pressure to her clit, which helped *loads*. Tension built and was amplified by his mouth sampling her skin. She couldn't hear her fractured breathing over the sound of her heart pounding in her ears. She quickened her pace and went rigid when her climax hit. She lurched forward and rode him hard, sinking her teeth into his shoulder as pleasure took over.

Her orgasm was still going when tipped her back on the bench. He braced her legs against his chest and fucked her hard. She clawed at him as her orgasm continued. When her vision cleared, she found him watching her, lion eyes eager and hungry.

"My turn."

He pulled out and flipped her so her legs straddled the bench and her hands splayed on the cushioned surface. He

positioned her the way he wanted before he impaled her
with a thrust that made her scream. He took her hard. She
grit her teeth and forced her trembling legs to hold her
while Gavin let his beast loose.

He jerked her head back so she looked at him in the
mirror while her hands stayed on the bench. The sight of
the muscled, dark beast dominating her small, pale form
made her mouth water. Her ass was up in the air, head
tipped back by the grip in her blond hair. Her body shuddered from the force of his thrusts. He was going so deep,
she knew she'd be feeling him tomorrow. Their eyes met in
the mirror. The possessive rage carving his face into
formidable lines made her even wetter.

"Who owns you?" he asked harshly.

"You."

"My name!"

"Gavin Pyre."

"And who do I belong to?"

She smiled through the pain. "Me."

His hand gripped her breast. "Who's your baby daddy?"

She rocked back against him. "You."

"That's right. Only me." He bent over her and buried
himself deep enough to make her eyes roll. "You ready to
breed, baby?"

2

HE RELEASED HIS GRIP ON HER HAIR. SHE DROPPED HER HEAD
forward and gripped the bench in preparation for what was
to come. When he ground himself against her, her toes
curled.

"You ready?" he murmured.

The force of his thrust sent her face first into the bench.
When her legs collapsed beneath the onslaught, his iron
grip held her up. She lay pliant before him, giving him what
he needed. Nothing else existed in her world except him. He
roared when he came. The force of his brutal thrust flat-
tened her. He dragged her limp form against him and
planted himself deep, groaning in her ear as she splayed on
the bench. Tears leaked out of her eyes because it was so
good. He shuddered and held her as close as possible as he
gave all of himself to her.

He collapsed against the reclined seat and draped her
over him. She panted against his chest and clung to him as
her throbbing body tried to recover. The smell of their
combined scents comforted her, and she floated on the
aftermath of amazing sex. His strong heart thumped

beneath her ear. He was her rock. They had their ups and downs, but it always came to this—their bond forged over a decade ago. Nothing could break it, and they were stronger now than they had ever been.

"We should spar more often," he said gruffly.

Her lips quirked as she stared at their reflection, her tiny form draped over the large warrior. "Next time, I get to win."

"If I win, you win too."

She couldn't refute his logic. "True."

His hand slid beneath the fall of her hair and cupped her nape. His strong fingers massaged while her breathing evened out. Gavin was right. There were other ways to work out her demons, but the bad thing was, at some point, her mind circled back to what caused her to feel like shit today. He couldn't fix this, but he had a right to know.

"I took Nora to see Mom," she said.

He didn't speak or stop his caressing.

"The nurses told me she hasn't been eating. I thought Nora would brighten her day since she's never met her before." Her chest tightened. She brushed her cheek over his skin, taking comfort in his presence before she said, "The minute she saw Nora, she went ballistic. She started screaming, throwing things, telling us to get out. It's the most she's talked in months."

She wasn't sure why Nora's presence triggered her mother, but it had, and not in a good way. She handed Nora to Blade and reentered the hospital room to find Beatrice trying to get out of bed. When she tried to stop her, Beatrice turned on her and tried to pummel her with her fists. Her mother actually hurt herself since she was weak and still in casts. Beatrice had to be restrained by the medical staff and sedated. Lyla emerged physically unscathed but mentally traumatized.

"She remembers," she whispered.

When her mother woke from the coma, no one knew how much she would remember. She hoped her mom would be spared that knowledge. No such luck. Today, Lyla had been introduced to an all new level of pain. She thought the worst thing in the world was seeing her mother strapped to a bed where she had been beaten to the brink of death. She was wrong. The worst thing in the world was seeing how much those monsters changed her mother into a bitter, enraged woman who couldn't stand the sight of her.

"She said she doesn't want to live with us ... and that it's my fault Dad's gone."

The worst part was, her mom was absolutely right. If only she knew the whole truth ... The shit that spewed out of Mom's mouth brought back everything she'd been trying to forget. She swallowed bile and buried her face against him.

"She asked where Pat's buried," she said against his skin.

"What did you say?"

"That he was killed by people in the underworld, and I don't know what they did with his body." She hesitated and then asked, "Did anyone go back to the cabin after ...?"

"Yes. He's buried near the cliff."

She wasn't sure how to feel about that.

"I shouldn't have let you see her without me," he said.

"It would have been the same outcome."

"I don't think so."

"She's changed." That was the understatement of the year.

"She has a right to act out, but not at you."

"I'm fine."

"You're not. You can't help her, so let the doctors and nurses do their job. We'll finance whatever she wants."

She nodded, recognizing the wisdom in that. She was going through her own shit and needed to take care of herself and Nora first before delving into her mother. She drank in Gavin's strength and willed his presence to chase away her feelings of guilt and helplessness.

When he straightened, she let out a disgruntled moan. He chuckled and gave her a swift kiss as he rose and settled her on the bench where she swayed before she found her balance. She watched him go to his pile of clothes and pull on his slacks.

"What am I going to wear? You ripped my shirt."

He tossed his dress shirt, which stopped at her knees. She eyed her pants, but they were too far away. He collected their clothes and her gun and circled back to her. When he eyed her expectantly, she lifted her arms and pouted, knowing he wouldn't deny her.

"Carry me?"

He reached for her. She knew what he was going to do before he did it.

"I don't want to be thrown over your shoulder. It hurts my stomach! I want a piggyback ride."

He looked at her blankly. "A piggy what?"

She got to her feet, and said, "Bend your knees."

She hopped on his back and wrapped her arms around his neck. He got the gist and supported her legs, which pointed straight ahead since he was too broad to wrap herself around.

"When Nora's old enough, she's gonna make you do this all the time," she said.

"Fine with me," he said.

"This is amazing. I'm over six feet tall."

She bounced against his back as they exited the gym. She kept a lookout for Blade, but he was nowhere to be found. Blade always made himself scarce when Gavin came home since he knew what a horny bastard he was.

"Everything okay at work?" she asked.

"Yes."

He climbed the stairs without effort. She rested her chin on his shoulder and nuzzled him.

"We should do this more often."

"Fuck in the gym?"

She thumped his shoulder. "Piggybacking."

"I'll give you piggybacks if you fuck me more."

"We fuck all the time, and this is supposed to be a couple's goals thing. This is the kind of stuff women post on social media to show how sweet their hubby is."

"We set our own goals, Lyla."

He turned into the nursery, tossed their belongings on a chair, and stopped beside the crib. She slipped down his back and held her breath as she peered down at their daughter. Nora was flat on her back, black hair covering half of her face. Nora was coming into her personality and loathed bows or hair ties with a passion. Her favorite stuffed animal right now was a pink elephant she never went anywhere without.

Lyla leaned down to pat their dogs, Beau and Honey, who shadowed Nora. Their tails thumped the ground as she fussed over them. She wouldn't admit it out loud, but it eased her mind knowing the dogs had appointed themselves as Nora's personal security. One could never have enough safeguards in place. When she saw Gavin reaching into the crib, she shot to her feet and smacked his arm.

"Do you want to wake her up?" she hissed.

"Yeah."

"No," she said firmly and pushed him out the door. "It's

almost one in the morning. You'll keep her up for hours, and her sleep schedule will be off."

Thankfully, he didn't fight her. When they entered their room, she slipped off his dress shirt and unwrapped her hands before she stepped into the shower. When he joined her, he slid her wedding ring on her finger. When she stood in front of the vanity to blow dry her hair, he came up behind her and wrapped his arms around her.

"Feel better?" he asked.

She nodded.

He kissed her cheek. "She'll heal. Give her time."

She watched him walk out of the bathroom. Since when did Gavin become a sage? He'd changed since they emerged from Hell. He was calm, confident ... satisfied? Like Carmen, he could move on now that Manny and Vinny had been avenged, but she couldn't. In her mind, it was only a matter of time before some other asshole rose up and tried to test them. Steven managed to put together an impressive committee of powerful men in the city. They had perished in Hell, but those men were part of organizations that opposed them and could cause trouble in the future. The Pyre name would always make them targets.

She blow-dried her hair and ran her hands through the shiny blond locks. Her mother used to have the same hair before it was shaved off. She looked at herself in the mirror. Her robe gaped, showing the gruesome scars on her chest. Her skin tingled as Steven's soft, malicious voice slithered through her mind.

You bear my mark, Lyla. What does Pyre think of that? I hope he thinks of me every time he touches you. The almighty Gavin Pyre brought to his knees by little old me.

She deliberately replayed her memory of crushing

Steven's bones with Lucifer's shield. He was dead. He couldn't hurt them anymore. "Fuck you, Steven."

Her scars were nothing compared to her mother's. Steven's men slashed Beatrice's skin to ribbons. Not an inch of her had been left untouched. It had been touch and go with her mom after one of her surgeries, but she had pulled through. Her mom was in significant pain and would be for the rest of her life. She lost one eye, and there had been significant damage to the other. Her mother's world had been shredded to pieces. Lyla had no clue how to be there for her mom, but after today, she knew it was best she kept her distance.

The crushing guilt was a physical weight on her chest. She couldn't catch her breath. She tilted her face up to the ceiling and focused on breathing past the panic clawing at her throat. A useless tear slid out of the corner of her eye. She couldn't change the past. All she could do was get through the present and focus on the future.

When she had herself back under control, she averted her gaze from the mirror and finished her nighttime routine. Maybe she should take a page out of Carmen's book and dye her hair or something, a declaration of a new beginning. Once Carmen found out Vinny had been avenged, she dyed her hair red and celebrated by partying her ass off. She wished she could be more like Gavin and Carmen. Gavin acted like the events in Hell never happened. He was as cool as a cucumber and slept like a baby while she was plagued by panic attacks and nightmares.

After she dressed in a nightgown, she walked into the room and found Gavin standing in front of the window, talking on his phone in Spanish. She went to check on Nora and collected her gun and clothes from the chair Gavin left them on. She rested her chin on the side of the crib and watched her daughter sleep. Her heart clenched. Nora was the best thing that ever happened to her. Locked in that cell in Hell, she thought she'd never see her daughter or Gavin ever again.

She chanced fate by stroking Nora's soft cheek. "You're safe, baby. Mommy's here." And she would do whatever it took to ensure Nora had a long, full life, even if it meant killing her father or anyone else who stood in her way.

Once more, she paused to love on Beau and Honey who were curled around each other. All of them had been through a lot. It was time for them to heal.

When she walked back into the master suite, Gavin was still on the phone. She set the gun on the nightstand and climbed in the bed on her side. She burrowed beneath the covers, comforted by the sound of his rumbling voice. There had been more than a few nights when Gavin was forced to work at night. Whether it was for the casino or underworld, she didn't know. All she cared about was that he came home to her whole and healthy.

She closed her eyes and took a deep breath. Fuck. The stupid shower invigorated her. She wasn't remotely sleepy. She stared at the ceiling as her fingers tapped on the blanket.

It's your fault your father is dead!

She flinched as her mother's accusation slid through her mind. It was her fault, all right. She pulled the fucking trigger... and she would do it again if she had to. As usual, the thought of Pat made her sick. She tensed, ready to make a run to the toilet. If Pat hadn't made a side deal, maybe her mother would have been saved from this horror. She rolled and buried her face in the pillow and tried to think of anything but him.

Gavin climbed into bed when he ended his call. She

turned toward him as he sat up with his back against the headboard and stretched out his legs.

"Trouble?" she asked.

"Nothing major."

That could mean anything, but she didn't push. She tossed an arm over his leg and rested her head on his thigh. It took less than three seconds for his hand to land on her hair, which brought up her earlier thought.

"I want to dye my hair."

His fingers paused. "What color?"

She pursed her lips. "Maybe a nice brown or something."

No response.

She looked up and saw his frown. "You're lucky I don't want pink hair."

"Fuck that." His fingers sifted through her hair. "I love your natural shade."

"I know. Maybe a haircut, then."

"A cut?"

She snickered. "It's not the end of the world, Gavin."

"I'd rather let you dye it green than cut it."

"Fine," she said, knowing that wasn't the end of it.

"Are you really thinking about green?" he asked a minute later.

She shrugged.

His fingers slipped through the strands. "Talk to me before you do anything."

She grunted.

"I'm serious."

Even as she considered different hair colors, a part of her knew she wouldn't do it. So much had changed that something simple like dyeing her hair could bring on a panic attack.

"What are you going to do when Nora wants purple hair?" She hoped Nora grew up with all the personality and zeal she never had.

"I can handle it."

Of course, he would handle it. He would do anything for Nora. That knowledge edged out her ambivalent feelings about her parents and filled her with warmth. Her daughter was loved and would grow up having the support and love she never received. Nora wouldn't have her insecurities.

She examined Gavin as he tapped on his phone. The image of her husband in a three-piece suit covered in blood with swords in each hand clashed with the man sitting up in bed writing emails on his phone. Lucifer called him a veteran of Hell … The fact that Gavin had once visited that evil place on a regular basis chilled her, but that wasn't him anymore. He was the boogie man of the underworld, but at the moment, he looked domesticated and, for the most part, harmless. He kept his word to her and got out of the under-world once he found a replacement. Since Manny and Vinny had been avenged, he seemed content with his lot in life. That was all that mattered, right?

"You're a good husband," she said.

"Of course, I am," he said without looking away from his phone.

She rolled her eyes. "Yes, you're the best unless you have to be sedated and thrown in the basement."

He stopped typing and his eyes narrowed on her.

"You drove me to the breaking point."

The lazy mood began to slip away as the reason for him being locked in the basement reflected in his eyes. Her ex coming back into the picture three months ago nearly broke them, and it was clearly still a sore spot. When she shifted to slip her head off his lap, he stopped her.

"Only two things could make me lose control," he said quietly.

"Jonathan."

The muscles in his thigh flexed. "Don't say his name."

"What's the other thing?"

His thumb dipped into the moist cavern of her mouth and rubbed saliva on her dry lips. His penetrating eyes bored into hers. "Leaving me."

"Oh." Well, that wouldn't happen. They were a unit. Psychotic, murderous episodes aside, she loved him. There were two things they hadn't agreed on—his position as crime lord and Jonathan—and neither of those was a factor any longer. Jonathan was now working for Gavin. As long as she knew he was still breathing, she didn't need to know all the details. Jonathan must have done some fast talking when Gavin went to Maine to—

"Lyla!"

She jolted. "What?" She was baffled by the banked rage in his eyes.

He gripped her face a bit too hard. "You're mine."

She scowled. "I know."

"He'll never be a part of your life."

Gavin went berserk when he caught her and Jonathan in a hotel room together. If Blade hadn't sedated him, who knew what he would have done?

Gavin's cold, golden eyes drifted over her face. "You threatened to leave me for him."

"No, I threatened to leave you if you killed him. He shouldn't have to pay with his life for being my friend."

"He was more than your friend."

The very mention of Jonathan made him homicidal. Gavin would spill blood to protect her and kill without mercy if she showed signs of love for someone he didn't deem worthy.

As if he could read her thoughts, he stroked her cheek with his thumb. "Careful who you give your affection to, wife."

She bristled. "I've always been careful. He's the only one I—"

His hand clamped over her mouth. *"Don't."*

She glared at him. He was such a dominant, macho, possessive bastard. His eyes held hers as he pulled her into a sitting position with effortless strength, one hand still gagging her as he positioned her sideways on his lap. She tried to jerk his hand off her mouth, but she stopped fighting when it tightened.

"We've been good for three months," he said.

She grunted through his paw. He leaned in close, lion eyes burning.

"Don't fuck it up," he warned.

Her eyes narrowed to slits. He allowed her to rip his hand from her mouth and watched her with an intensity that told her he was ready to pounce.

"Don't threaten me, Gavin. I haven't done anything!"

"You brought up that fuck," he growled.

"I brought up what a psycho you are. *You* brought up Jona—" She was cut off when his hand clapped over her mouth again.

"What did I say?" he hissed.

She glared balefully at him.

"Even if I was dead and buried, you wouldn't have a chance in hell of going back to him."

She bit his palm and yanked his hand down. "How would you stop me if you're dead?"

He didn't answer; he just watched her. She tried to think

like her husband. It was a difficult task because she didn't have the faintest idea how his mind worked. He was a master strategist and ruthless crime lord. She didn't have the years of experience in war and manipulation that he did. Even now, she couldn't predict his reactions to topics. Case in point, her current position on his lap with his mouth on her chin, ready to silence her if she said something he didn't like. She considered Gavin for several minutes before it clicked.

"You wouldn't ..." she whispered. "You did *not* give Blade orders to ..." No change in expression, which was answer enough. "You put Blade on cock block duty for the rest of his life? Are you crazy?"

"He'll never get to you."

"He doesn't even *want* to get to me," she exploded.

"He does."

"He doesn't have a chance with me. I explained that to him."

His hand slipped beneath her nightgown, slid over her thighs, and glided up to her pussy. She didn't bother to wear underwear to bed since he'd rip them off anyway.

"I don't want you to be happy without me," he declared.

He had no qualms stating what he wanted. He didn't care how it made him look or what others thought. He was blunt, jealous, and relentless about his claim on her.

"What about Nora?" she asked indignantly.

"She has godfathers."

"And I get nothing?"

"Your memories of me will be enough. No one could fill my shoes."

"I can't believe you made plans for me even if you're dead."

"Why wouldn't I?"

It was so fucking Gavin that all she could do was shake her head. "You're obsessed with me." This thought had crossed her mind more than once throughout the years but knowing how much he'd planned in advance really drove that thought home. He wouldn't let go of her even in death.

"Only now you realize I'm obsessed with you?"

"I know you are, but you're, like, over the top."

He tugged her head back and pressed gentle kisses over her throat. "I'm making sure what's mine stays mine."

She should be more pissed off that he would manipulate her life from the grave, but it was hard to focus when he was sucking on her neck. To some degree, he was right. No one would ever measure up to him, and how could she go from his absolute possession to anything lukewarm and sweet?

You're in the underworld where men mark their women by carving or tattooing their initials on her face. Blade's words drifted through her mind as Gavin marked her. Gavin claimed her in every way possible, but he hadn't pushed her to get a brand. How would he react if she got a tattoo for him? He would lose his fucking mind in the best way.

He kissed her long and deep. She cupped his face and loved him back. His hands moved restlessly beneath her gown, and she spread her thighs when he growled. She gripped a handful of his hair and pulled back so she could see his face.

"Why do you love me?"

It was a question that plagued her throughout the day. If she told Beatrice the truth about Pat, her mother would condemn her for life. It didn't matter what her father did. He would get a pass, as he always had. She, on the other hand, would be deemed unforgivable.

Witnessing her mother's tormented distress hurt her soul. Beatrice didn't want to live. The nurses said her mother refused physical therapy, which was why she had visited today. Beatrice was being monitored closely because of some recent, disturbing outbursts. It was a good thing her mother would be going into her own home. Maybe she would heal better in a place with her things around her ... or not. With Pat gone, her mom didn't see any reason to get better. The fact that her mom still had a daughter who would care for her and a grandbaby she had yet to meet meant nothing to her.

She risked her life and the lives of Gavin's men to free Beatrice. She remembered that horrible drive—gripping the steering wheel for dear life and refusing to believe she was too late. The fact that her mother lived through such brutal torture was a miracle. The fact she breathed and could now scream at her was a fucking miracle. Beatrice had been given a chance to build a new life, one free of a husband who had never put her first, but she didn't want it. It hammered home how grossly inadequate Lyla had always felt. It's why she clung to the Pyres, who acted as if she was something special. This brutal, ruthless man loved her when her parents never had. Why?

Gavin's brows bunched together. "What are you talking about?"

"Why do you love me?" she asked with more force than was necessary.

"Because you love monsters."

He nuzzled her as if she was a cute puppy. She smacked his cheek and shoved away. He wasn't taking her seriously when she needed a real answer. She slipped off his lap and received a sharp push that landed her flat on her back with him looming over her. The soft mattress made it easy for her to knock him off balance and pin *him*. He laughed, which pissed her off.

She bared her teeth at him. "I should elbow you in the throat."

He didn't look angry that she was threatening him bodily harm. On the contrary, he looked delighted.

"If you do that, I get anal."

Her glare should have made him wither on the spot. "Fuck you, Gavin."

She tried to push off, but his grip on her nape kept her in place above him.

"You want to know why I love you," he said, and she stopped fighting. "You're the innocent lamb who gravitated to the most dangerous men in the city." He smiled as he lifted the back of her nightgown and gripped her ass. "You liked Dad at his worst. You saw him as a harmless old man. You brought him back from the brink and made him believe in something besides death. You saw what you wanted to see in us, and we were happy to give you the illusion."

She didn't like the sound of that but couldn't deny it was true.

"I liked your innocence for the same reason Dad did. You weren't a part of our world, and you gave us a place where we could be ourselves. I convinced myself that I couldn't be such a bastard if someone like you loved me." His hands stopped their playful wandering and pressed on her lower back, flattening her on top of him. "When you left, there was no buffer between me and the world. I didn't need to pretend for you, so I became who I really am."

"You said you loved me because of my innocence," she said quietly.

He nodded.

"I'm not innocent anymore."

He considered her thoughtfully.

"So why do you love me?" she whispered.

"I fell for the innocent and was obsessed with getting you back so you could make me believe I could be a better man, but you're innocent only once in life. Once it's ruined, it's gone forever."

"Yes." She'd never been the same after witnessing what Gavin was capable of.

"This is gonna sound fucked up, but I like that I'm the one who took that from you." His hand quested down her spine, between her ass, straight to the heart of her. "I took your virginity, your heart, your mind. Mine." The hand on her nape flexed. "I changed the way you see the world. I took the rose-colored glasses from your eyes and forced you to see me as I am. Sometimes I think you'll run from me again." He rolled until she was beneath him and placed his palm over her left breast. "But I have this. I put my stamp on it. It beats for me."

"Yes," she whispered. No matter how far she ran, he would catch up to her. She wasn't sure what connected a girl from a middle-class family to a crime lord, but the connection was there, unbreakable.

"I loved the innocent because she helped me believe the lie, but I love the woman because she made me accept who I am."

He sat up and dragged off her nightgown. She didn't fight him. He draped her thighs over his and stared at her body for long moments before he freed himself and pressed for entry. She was wet enough to take him but just barely. He didn't stop until he was in to the hilt. He stroked her belly and then her chest, over the scars.

"I'm a monster. I'll do whatever it takes to keep my family safe, to keep the dogs at bay. No mercy, no second chances." He placed a dry kiss on her lips and pulled back, eyes searching hers. "You know what's in me, yet you ask me for piggyback rides. You challenge me, showing no fear. That's why I love you. You're my anchor, my partner, my mate, my badass." His hand moved over her stomach. "You're giving me a legacy, a love that will never run dry. If you think I'd leave any room for you to wiggle out of, you're dead wrong."

She let out a choked laugh and rested her forehead against his. "You scare the fuck out of me sometimes, but most of the time, I love the way you love me."

"And how's that?"

"Like a fucking monster."

3

LYLA SAT ON A LOUNGER BESIDE THE POOL IN HER BACKYARD. The sound of the waterfall and the light of the sun bouncing off the water were relaxing. It was unusually quiet, but she wasn't alarmed. Her eyes moved over the mountains she had stared at so many times before. Something was different about them, but she couldn't put her finger on what.

"Hey, baby girl."

She turned her head. Manny Pyre lay on the lounger beside her in bright red shorts and an awful Aloha shirt decorated with blue flamingoes. The shirt was unbuttoned, showing a chest and stomach covered in snow white hair. He wore a straw fedora and oversized shades. He was a sight for sore eyes. Her heart swelled with so much emotion that she couldn't breathe. The only way to release the pressure was through the tears that slipped down her cheek. She tried to reach for him, but her body was heavy and unresponsive. She didn't fight it. Instead, she drank him in. His smile lit up her world.

"How's life, baby girl?"

She smiled through the tears. "Better now. How are you, Manny?"

He pulled down his shades and eyed her. "Better than you."

She let out a weak laugh. "I bet. Life hasn't been smooth sailing lately."

"No, and it never will be." He wriggled his toes and tipped his face up to the sun. "There's always going to be another wave, another battle. Take what you can get. God gives you pockets of time to enjoy and regroup, so take advantage and don't squander it. Life is too short."

She stared at the shimmering water as the sun beat down on them. "Yes, we need a break. Maybe we should get out of the city."

"You should. Your first family vacation."

That brought her attention back to him. A shaft of sorrow cut through her joy. "Have you seen her?"

Manny pressed his hand against his chest. "Nora's perfect, just as I knew she would be."

She swallowed hard as another tear slipped down her face. "I-I wish you could meet her. She'd love you."

"I will one day. Until then, I get to watch over her." He grinned roguishly. "She's gonna be entertaining, that one. She's gonna lead the pack, a born leader. Teach her to trust her heart and she'll never go wrong. The others will follow her lead."

"Others?" she echoed.

He tilted his head back and laughed. The wonderful sound tickled her ears and invited her to join in. The compulsion to touch him intensified. A part of her knew this was a dream, but she didn't care. Touching him was paramount. She wanted nothing more than to feel him, warm and solid, just for a moment. As she willed her body to move, Manny's image blurred. She felt herself drifting between wakefulness and sleep and instantly stilled. She was relieved when Manny snapped back into focus.

"You have no idea," he said, unaffected by her consciousness. "Your life's just getting started, baby girl. The best is yet to come."

"Really?"

He nodded curtly. "You have years ahead of you full of ups and downs, but you're gonna make it. No matter how bad life is, it keeps moving, and so do you."

She felt the intensity of his gaze through the dark shades.

"You done good, baby girl. You avenged me."

She ignored the prickle of unease that slithered down her spine. "Yes, Manny, he's gone." Her eyes moved over his body, which was unblemished, as it had been before his murder.

He drew his shades down again to eye her sternly. "I don't want you to remember how I died."

Her chest ached. "I can't help it. I should have—"

"There was nothing you could do." He sighed and waved his hand, causing his gaudy rings to sparkle. "I'm a bad man, baby girl. I've done things you wouldn't believe. I had it coming. Every man who takes a place in the underworld knows what we're courting, and it caught up to me. I just regret you had to witness it. You shouldn't have been there for that."

"It's over, Manny."

He nodded. "It is. Vengeance was served, and you and Gavin are starting a new chapter. You're two halves of the same whole. You're both strong in different ways. You're good for each other. Your path isn't an easy one, but you have friends and family to help you through the dark times.

As a unit you're invincible. Trust each other and you'll pull through."

She heard a noise in the distance and knew instinctively it was from the waking world, a world she didn't want to return to yet. She focused on him with every fiber of her being. This dream was so precious, she would give anything for more time.

"You finally let yourself love him the way he needs, the way I never could. I did things to him you wouldn't agree with, but it was for the best. He wouldn't be who he is today without his training, and I don't regret it. He's a man who will never give up, which is what he needs to survive."

Manny stared at her with his son's piercing gaze.

"You have no idea what's coming."

"What do you mean?"

"Be strong for me, baby girl. You can take it."

"I don't understand."

He spoke faster. "Don't be afraid to ask for help. You know who you can trust. Keep them close. Create the family you need."

His image began to blur, and the fear of losing him rose up again, choking her.

"Wait, don't leave me," she begged and fought the paralysis as the colors of her world began to bleed.

"I'll never leave you. You were always my light, Lyla. Shine bright."

4

Lyla lurched up in bed, hands outstretched, tears rolling down her cheeks. She knew without opening her eyes that she wasn't by the pool. She was in bed in the master suite with the rumpled sheets wrapped around her naked body. She dropped her face in her hands and sobbed. It was like losing him all over again. Manny was the first person to see something special in her. He gave her the confidence to express her opinions and listened to her when everyone else had ignored her. He was an integral part of her life, her father in every way but blood, and he was gone like so many others.

She rolled out of bed and splashed water on her face before she dressed in mommy attire—yoga pants and another oversized shirt. When she found the nursery empty, she trotted downstairs. Her somber mood lightened considerably when she found Gavin on the floor with Nora in the living room. Nora scooted determinedly while Honey and Beau watched avidly.

Gavin looked up with a smile that made her heart sore. Like father, like son. Manny was right. Gavin was happy.

Happier than she could ever remember him being, even when they were together before. Back then, he'd been so guarded and mired in deception and underworld shit and now ... Now, he was just himself. CEO, husband, father, and it looked fucking amazing on him.

"Morning, baby," he said.

She went to him and kissed him. "Thanks for letting me sleep. You're not going to work today?"

"No, I'm taking the day off."

She scooped up Nora who wasn't happy about being interrupted during her crawling attempts. She pet the dogs and ambled into the kitchen. As she made herself a cup of tea, her gaze wandered outside to the pool where the sun highlighted the red and gold striped loungers she and Manny had been on. She couldn't help herself. She walked outside and looked around, almost expecting him to appear out of thin air. Everything was just as it had been in the dream. She sat on the lounger Manny occupied and closed her eyes. It was warm from the sun, but she imagined it was from his body heat, as if he had just walked away. Wistful longing laced with heartache filled her, and her breath hitched.

She felt a whoosh of air as a furry body burrowed between her legs. Beau rested his chin on her ankle and sighed loudly. He was never far from her when she was having a hard day. He knew her moods better than she did. She sent her hand through his fur and let the anguish drain slowly. She wasn't sure whether the dream was a blessing or a curse and didn't care. The sorrow was worth the price of seeing him. She hadn't had a dream like that since before Nora was born. Though it had been three years since his death, it felt like yesterday. Fuck, she missed him.

A psychologist would tell her that it was her subconscious supplying these fantasies and that her mixed feelings about her father caused her to conjure the only loving parental figure she had. Did it really matter why she dreamed of Manny? If her brain wanted to create an illusion where Manny encouraged her to move forward, love her family, and forgive herself, why shouldn't she? She wanted to believe that Manny was at peace and watching over them. It was the only thing she would accept.

When she went in the house, she found Nora perched in a baby seat on the kitchen island. Gavin had cereal smeared on his shirt and was trying to feed his daughter who kept grabbing the spoon before he could reach her mouth.

"You okay?" he asked.

She wrapped her arms around him from behind and sighed. "Yeah."

She drew in his scent and grinned. His cologne was overpowered by the smell of baby powder.

"Let's go out of town," she said.

Manny was right. She had to stop hiding in the house, waiting for the next shitstorm. Traveling would distract her from her worries and snap her out of her melancholy.

"We can go wherever you want," Gavin said.

"Really?"

"Anywhere. France? Greece? Japan?"

"I want quiet, no crowds."

"Mountains or beach?"

She peeked around him and eyed Nora. "Sand."

"I'll take care of it."

"Thank you." She squeezed him and ran her hands over his toned stomach, allowing her hands to dip past his waistline. She grinned wickedly when his muscles flexed. He whipped his head around to look at her.

"What are you doing?" he rumbled.

She gave him a guileless look. "Nothing." She took the cereal from him. "You need to make some calls?"

"Yeah," he said distractedly.

"Go ahead. I can take it from here." She widened her eyes at Nora who mimicked her and then babbled excitedly. She ignored Gavin who watched her for a full minute before he stalked from the room. Gavin reacted so beautifully to her. No matter how small her come on was, he noticed immediately. She had never been the aggressor at any time in their relationship, and there was no way she could ever be, but she could do other things ... Like rile him up with deceivingly innocent touches and act oblivious about her effect on him.

"How's my baby girl?" she cooed.

Nora smacked her hands against her rubber seat and shouted at the top of her lungs. As a natural blonde, she was fascinated by her daughter's jet-black hair. She secretly hoped Nora's hair would always have a hint of curl. Nora's animated silver blue eyes shimmered with curiosity. Her round cheeks were rosy with color and even though her face was covered with cereal, Lyla couldn't resist. She covered Nora's face in loud, smacking kisses that caused her to scream in delight.

After breakfast, she decided Nora needed a sponge bath. The dogs accompanied her and licked Nora's toes when they could. After putting Nora in a new outfit, she nabbed her phone and settled on the floor in the nursery as Nora scooted around, surrounded by a ridiculous number of bright toys.

A call to the hospital to check on her mom revealed that she'd been sedated in the middle of the night. Beatrice had an episode and damaged some machines. Lyla stared at Nora who faced Beau. He lay on his belly, watching her with adoring eyes. Honey paced around the perimeter, watching her warily. Apparently, Honey sensed her mood change. Lyla gave her a reassuring smile and swallowed the lump in her throat.

"Do you think I should come down?" Just last night, she agreed to stay away from her mother, but if she needed her ...

"Personally, Mrs. Pyre, I think it's best that you take a break. I know you're a new mom, and after what happened yesterday ... I think she needs to rest with no visitors or other stimulation."

The relief she felt made her feel like a crap daughter. "Okay, please keep me updated."

"Will do. You have a great day now."

Lyla lowered the phone and stared at it. Whatever the nurse told her was definitely watered down. She let out a long breath and dialed Carmen who didn't answer. Carmen moving out of the house had been hard for her. She was her best friend, cousin, and sister all rolled into one bundle of crazy. Carmen's support had been invaluable when Nora was born... and during all the crazy shit that had happened since. No one could replace her. Although she wished her cousin was with her every day, she could see Carmen needed to move forward with her life. And damn, she grabbed the bull by the horns. Carmen had moved in with Marcus. Seeing her cousin in a relationship after all these years was a miracle. Marcus was a good man, one who Lyla believed could help Carmen heal. If Carmen ended up breaking his heart, she'd have to kick her cousin's ass.

Nora screamed when she couldn't reach one of her toys beneath a chair. Lyla retrieved it before the sound of his daughter's distressed cry brought Gavin upstairs. She gave Nora the toy and plopped the baby in her lap. There was

unavoidable pain in life, but there was also unspeakable
beauty. She held it between her hands. Nora slobbered over
her toy and stared at her with inquiring eyes. *She's gonna
lead the pack, a born leader.* Manny had predicted what she
already knew. The independent tendencies Nora was
exhibiting at such an early age were freaking her out. Nora
was definitely Gavin's daughter. He was so proud of her
headstrong ways. She wanted to put Nora in bubble wrap
and protect her for as long as she could, but she knew life
would find her. All she could do was love her to make the
hard times hurt less. She hugged Nora to her. Her daughter
allowed this for a moment before she pushed off and abandoned one toy for another.

When her phone rang, she picked it up immediately.
"Hey."

"What's up, chick?" Carmen asked.

She rubbed her temples. "Oh, you know, just trying to be
a ray of sunshine."

"How's that working for you?"

"Not well."

"You want to go to a dance class? It's super dirty, way
worse than my pole class. We fuck the shit out of these
chairs."

Lyla snickered. "I hope they sanitize the chairs after
each class."

"No. That's why I like it."

"You're gross."

Carmen laughed. "I know."

"I think I'll pass today. Gavin's home."

"Good. Get some nookie and report back."

"I got some last night."

Carmen hummed. "Nice."

She relaxed. Carmen's teasing never failed to lighten her mood. "There was boxing involved."

"Go on."

"And a weight bench."

"I think Marcus needs a home gym," Carmen said thoughtfully, and Lyla grinned. "Hey, I'm pulling up to the class now. I'll call you tomorrow, okay? Lunch?"

"Yeah, that sounds good."

"Okay, love you."

"You too, bye."

Lyla tidied up the nursery and kept an eye on Nora who had an unhealthy obsession with the carpet and kept trying to lick it. Beau followed her around and bumped his nose on the back of her leg for attention while Honey observed. Honey was a recent rescue she stole from Carmen. For the most part, Honey seemed to be adapting well. She'd regressed several times to a timid state, but Lyla wasn't bothered. She hadn't adapted well from things in her past. She stopped what she was doing to pull Nora away from the chair leg she was gnawing on.

When Nora was ready for a nap, she decided she needed one too. The dogs followed her into the master suite and climbed on the bed. She curled around Nora and stroked her hair. Nora's long lashes fanned her face as she fought sleep. Lyla grinned as her daughter tried to roll away from her. She brought her back into place and continued to stroke her hair until Nora gave in with a scowl.

"Don't be in such a rush, baby girl," she murmured as she rested her cheek on her hands and watched her baby sleep.

Knowing Gavin was near allowed her to drift off much easier than her daughter. She woke an hour later to Nora's hungry howl. She changed her before they trooped downstairs with the dogs rushing ahead of her and dashing out to the backyard. After she fed Nora, she made herself a sandwich and was halfway through it when she realized something was wrong. With Nora on her hip, she walked into Gavin's office.

"Where's Blade?" she asked.

Gavin rose from his desk, took Nora, and gave her a quick kiss. "He needed to do something."

She stared at him. "Do something? What does that mean? Is that why you took the day off?"

"Yeah."

She followed him into the kitchen where he finished her sandwich while fending off Nora's seeking hands. "What is he doing?"

"Does it matter?"

She put her hands on her hips. "Uh, *yeah.*"

"Why?"

"Because ..." She struggled to find a reason why Blade's disappearance disturbed her so much. "He's never left me before." If she hadn't been so distracted by the dream of Manny, she would have noticed much sooner.

Gavin dug around in the fridge. "He'll be back."

"When?"

He gave her an odd look. "What's the big deal?"

"The big deal is he's my shadow, and he's here day and night. Is there something wrong with him? Did he have to go to the doctor or something?"

"Don't be dramatic, Lyla."

Her eyes narrowed. "I'm not being dramatic. I just want to know where he is. Why won't you tell me?"

"I'll let him decide what to tell you when he gets back."

"And when does he get back?"

He cocked his head to the side. Nora copied him, which

almost made her laugh, but she was too preoccupied with Blade's whereabouts.

"You don't get like this when I leave you," Gavin observed.

"Because you have to leave me. You need to run Pyre Casinos and kill people. Blade doesn't. I'm his job, right?"

"You're his main priority, but he has other tasks."

"That come before me?"

"Of course not."

"Then where is he?"

"Give it up, Lyla."

She waved her hands. "That's not fair. He's on my ass all day, telling me to work out or when to sleep or eat. He's like you, but nicer."

He scowled. "What?"

"He's my shadow. He should tell me he's gonna leave me."

"You don't need to know," he said and patted her butt before he grabbed a flaky croissant.

"Gavin!"

"Here."

He held his phone out to her. She took it and stared at the screen, which had an image of an island on it.

"What's this?"

"Bora Bora. I think you'll like it."

She flipped through the images of white sand beaches and crystal-clear waters and was convinced within two minutes that this is exactly where they needed to be. "It's gorgeous. When are we going?"

"Couple of weeks. It'll give me enough time to take care of things at work and make sure Angel's good."

She looked up quickly. "Why? Is something wrong?"

Gavin glanced at Nora, who was watching them intently.

It was almost as if she could understand what they were saying.

"It'll take time for the underworld to accept him, so I'm just biding my time and showing my support."

"And how are you doing that?"

The monster looked back at her. "The way I've always done it."

"Are the Black Vipers taken care of?"

Aside from that mishap with the Black Vipers, Angel seemed to be doing well as crime lord. She saw the fear and dread on Gavin's face when he got the call because it was history replaying itself. Another cousin filling his shoes nearly gunned down. Gavin had spent some nights out with Angel. She didn't question him at the time because she knew he was ensuring his cousin's well-being. Whatever Angel needed, they'd provide. The fact that Angel was willing to take on the underworld after witnessing the damage Steven wrought on the city was mind-boggling. She shouldn't be surprised, though. He was a Roman and ruling was in his blood, same as Gavin.

"It'll take some time before they're contained," Gavin said.

He bit into an apple and continued to talk, but she was distracted by his fitted jeans. He should dress down more often. He wore a soft gray shirt that clung to his biceps. He looked more like a bodybuilder than a CEO. Maybe when Blade came home, he could babysit Nora, and they could box ...

"Is Blade doing something for Angel? Is that why you won't tell me where he is?" she asked.

Gavin tossed his apple core and shook his head. "You're obsessing."

"I learned from the master," she retorted.

"If only you were this interested in my whereabouts."

"Seventy percent of the time, you're at work. Ten percent, you do underworld stuff, and the other twenty, you're with us." She grit her teeth when he dug in the fridge for something else to eat. "You know, it's not fair that you guys can track and spy on me anytime and you won't even tell me where he is."

The sound of the front door closing shut her up. Seconds later, Blade entered the kitchen with a black bag slung over one shoulder.

"He left *last night,* and you didn't tell me?" she snapped at Gavin.

"Christ," he growled. "What does it matter?"

"It matters because we could have been attacked, and I didn't even know he wasn't here!"

"You know," Gavin drawled. "I know how to use a gun too."

"That's not the point." She walked up to Blade and smacked his chest with her palm. "And where were you?"

Blade looked from her to Gavin and back. "What the hell?"

"You just take off without telling me?"

Blade dropped his bag and went to Nora who was going wild in Gavin's arms. Blade held the baby against his chest and ignored Nora's attempts to kiss him. Lyla took in his appearance. Like Gavin, he was dressed down. Dark jeans and shirt with an army green jacket. He got a haircut, and while his normally stony expression was still foreboding, something was different about him.

"Where have you been?" she asked.

"Why?"

How many times did she need to repeat herself? "You've never left me before."

Blade flicked a glance at Gavin before he said, "You weren't in danger."

"How would you know? You weren't here!"

"Lyla." Gavin's tone was chiding as he built two massive sandwiches.

Blade frowned. "Did you have an episode today?"

She crossed her arms. "No!"

"Then what are you so ticked off about?"

"I should know when you're going to leave me."

"Why?"

"Because." Both men were staring at her as if she lost her mind. "You're my constant."

"Your what?" Gavin asked.

She waved her hands as she tried to make them understand. "I know Gavin has to go to work. Carmen moved out, and the only person who's always here is Blade."

He started off as a gruff second in command, but somewhere along the road, he had morphed into something else. He was her protector, teacher, trainer, confidant, and shadow. He was such an intrinsic part of her life that his disappearance made her feel as if something vital was missing.

"You're by my side day and night for three years. You can't just vanish into thin air! What if I need you?"

There was a humming silence in the kitchen. She was dimly aware of the weight of Gavin's stare, but she didn't look at him. Her focus was on Blade who was watching her with a grim, contemplative expression.

"I know you can't be with me twenty-four seven, but can you ... can you just tell me when you're going somewhere?" she asked.

Blade nodded. "I can do that."

She let out a long breath. "Thank you." She finally

chanced a look at Gavin to find him shaking his head. She was glad he wasn't going to Hulk out about her attachment to Blade that she hadn't even been aware of. How could she not depend on him? He was there for every crisis, taking charge and putting his life in jeopardy without hesitation. They had fought side by side. He saw her and Gavin at their worst and never strayed from her side. Blade was an immovable force that had never let her down.

"So where did you go?" she asked.

"None of your business."

She scowled. He was annoying as hell. When he passed her, she caught a faint whiff of heavy perfume. "You're seeing someone?"

Blade put Nora in her high chair and ignored her.

"You have a girlfriend?" she persisted.

Blade sneered. "Never had a girlfriend in my life."

"Booty call?"

"I never fuck the same girl more than once."

"So you got laid? That's it? Why'd you want to keep that from me? Did you go to the brothel in Crystal?"

Gavin straightened. "What the fuck?"

Blade looked bewildered. "Why would I drive to Crystal for whores when there's free pussy in the city?"

"Did you spend the whole night with your one-night stand?"

"You're done," Gavin announced as he grabbed her arm and towed her away from Blade who looked more displeased than usual. "How the hell do you know about Crystal?"

"Carmen and I drove out to the Love Ranch once."

A muscle clenched in his cheek. "Why?"

"Why not? Who wouldn't want to see a brothel? Did you

know the Love Ranch has a gift shop? The food isn't bad either."

"You *ate* there?"

"The staff was really nice. It says on the sign that sex isn't required. Some people go there for the food."

"I bet they do," he muttered.

He pulled her into his office and set her on the edge of his desk.

"Where the fuck was I when you went on this field trip?" he asked as he spread her legs to make a place for himself.

"At work."

"I should kill Carmen," he said as his hand slipped beneath her shirt.

She took great pleasure in throwing his words back in his face. "Oh, Gavin, don't be so dramatic."

"You should stop seeing her," he said as he cupped her breast.

"As if that would ever happen. She's my best friend."

His expression was inscrutable as he murmured, "Sounds like Blade's your best friend."

"Blade is ... I don't know what he is, but he's a part of us now." Blade wasn't necessarily a brother to her. He was caught somewhere between best guy friend and disapproving uncle.

He rested his forehead against hers as his hands continued to stroke her skin beneath her shirt. She looped her arms around his neck and closed her eyes as he cherished her without saying a word. There had been a lot of these moments in the past three months. Both of them knew how close they'd been to death. She drank him in, cupping his face before letting her fingers trace the strong line of his throat and then coming to rest over his heart.

"Are you happy?" she murmured, feeling drunk from his petting.

"You have doubts?"

I did things to him you wouldn't agree with. Manny's voice echoed in her mind as she opened her eyes and stared into his. "Just checking."

He raised her chin so he could kiss her slow and sweet. She arched against him as he teased her. When their lips parted, he surveyed her with heavy lidded eyes.

"I have you and Nora. I don't care about anything else."

To him, it was that simple. This man battled to keep her at his side and bonded her to him so tightly, she couldn't imagine life without him.

"I love you," she said.

He buried his face in the crook of her neck and breathed deep.

"Whatever you want, Lyla, it's yours," he said gruffly.

She wrapped her arms around him and held on tight. "I have what I want." How could she not love this psycho?

"I'm going to give you more," he vowed.

"You can't give me more than you have already."

He placed his lips on her ear as he said, "Watch me."

5

ONE MONTH LATER

GAVIN SURVEYED HIS COUSIN WHO SAT ON THE OPPOSITE SIDE of his desk. Three months as the crime lord of Las Vegas had taken a toll on Angel Roman. The smile on his face no longer reached his blue eyes. His hair was wet from a recent shower since he arrived in a blood-stained suit. Angel was forced to put on jeans and a shirt, a staple of his that Gavin could see didn't sit well with him anymore. He understood the feeling. Crime lords had an image to maintain, and the suit was a part of it. It became their uniform and a symbol of wealth, dominance, and authority. It didn't hurt that it concealed weapons and bloodstains. Suits were so versatile.

"Trouble?" he asked.

"A minor inconvenience," Angel said.

He was itching for action. Angel didn't betray himself by fidgeting or letting his attention wander restlessly around the office, but Gavin sensed it. The high of power and violence was a drug he was well acquainted with. It was what drove him to Hell and infidelity. The darkness of the underworld was making an impact on his younger cousin.

Angel was handling it well, but if he didn't find an outlet, it would drag him under.

Angel had adapted amazingly well. While he sneered at New York underworld traditions and politics, there was something to be said for having protocols in place. Las Vegas had turned into Gotham—lawless, pitiless, and brutal. Angel was morphing into his own brand of crime lord. He was deceptively accommodating until crossed. His methods to gain compliance were inspired. Word was spreading through the underworld of its new master.

He worked hand in hand with his cousin, adding his influence when necessary to solidify Angel's reign. He had to admit Angel was the best man for the job and kept Raul apprised of his brother's progress. Raul wasn't surprised by his younger brother's success. Resigned was more like it.

"Progress with the Black Vipers?" Gavin asked.

Angel overplayed his hand and barely survived a murder attempt. They had left a staggering number of bodies in the wake of that incident to make a statement. Any opposition would be removed. Since Raul sent reinforcements from New York, there hadn't been anymore close calls.

"The Black Vipers called on some California gangs, which have caused trouble, but we're taking care of it." Angel tilted his head to the side. "I hear some cops visited you at the casino."

"Their third visit since Malone and the others went missing. They showed up here once."

Angel's eyes narrowed. "They came to your residence?"

"They didn't make it past the gate. They were ... persuaded to leave."

Angel's mouth twitched. "Imagine that. So did they come right out and ask if you had anything to do with all these disappearances?"

He settled back in his chair. "They start with bullshit and then ask if I knew the governor and the gaming commissioner and so on." He was actually enjoying these verbal spars. The public was in an uproar over having so many public servants and government officials disappear into thin air. The cops were grasping at straws, hoping he'd slip up or some stupid shit. Everyone knew something big had gone down, but they didn't know where it took place or who was involved. The cops were smart enough to sniff around him, but they wouldn't find shit.

"I've been approached by some dirty cops. Looks like they want to make a deal with me," Angel said.

"You ask Stark about them?"

Angel nodded. "We declined their offer."

"How'd they take it?"

Angel's smile wasn't friendly. "They weren't happy, but they're smart enough to walk away with their tail between their legs."

"How's Stark working out?"

"He doesn't say much, but he knows his shit."

He felt better knowing that Stark had Angel's back. Stark knew the underworld well. Angel needed someone on hand who could help him make intelligent, split-second decisions. He also hoped Stark would curb Angel from doing anything too reckless.

"While I'm gone, if you need anything—"

Angel waved his hand. "Don't go all big cousin on me now."

"I can't resist." Reconnecting with his cousins was one of the best decisions he'd made. He had support, backup, and could give Lyla the life he always promised. "I owe you."

"For what? Gift wrapping the greatest city in the world for me?"

"It's dangerous."

"So am I."

He had underestimated his pretty boy cousin. Angel still had a ways to go before becoming a full-fledged crime lord, but he was holding his own in a world where only the strong survived.

"Go on your trip. I'll take care of everything." Angel sniffed the air appreciatively. "What's the occasion, anyway?"

"It's been four months since we killed that fuck."

Angel's eyes gleamed. "I should visit Hell, maybe piss in a toilet there as an extra fuck you to that little bastard."

"You heard from Lucifer?"

"No. Why?"

"Just checking." It wouldn't surprise him if Lucifer tried to reel Angel in. Angel put on a show in the pit to stake his claim as crime lord. Lucifer wouldn't fail to notice his skill.

He glanced down at the dog flopped on his foot. For some reason he couldn't fathom, Honey had taken a liking to him. She had become a permanent fixture in his office and followed him everywhere.

"That guy, Jonathan, came by my place," Angel said. "He installed the security system. It's amazing."

"What do you think of him?"

Angel shrugged. "He seemed a little nervous, but otherwise, fine. Smart guy. Why?"

"No reason." He hadn't had contact with Huskin since Maine. He gave his orders to Z who passed them onto Huskin. It was better that way. "He'll be installing our system while we're gone." There was no way in hell he would allow Huskin in the house with Lyla around. Their trip to Bora Bora was a convenient excuse for Huskin to come in and do his thing.

"You have some interesting contacts," Angel said.

"They come in handy," he said as he got to his feet.

"Don't worry about the city, Gav. I got it."

"Good. Then maybe you can get Luci to stop calling me every day."

Angel grinned as they exited the office. "She's going stir-crazy. I may have to let her come here for a weekend or something before she does something stupid."

He didn't like the thought of Luci coming here when things were still in transition, but it was Angel's call.

They passed the kitchen, which was filled with catering staff. He didn't like having strangers in his home. It put him on edge, but he could tolerate it for a few hours. There was a fancy table set up beside the pool. Lyla chatted with Carmen's mother, Isabel. He assumed the older man and teenager with her were the Armstrongs, the family she would be marrying into. He had looked into them and found they were as vanilla as could be, lucky for them.

He walked toward Lyla who turned when she sensed his approach. When she saw him, she smiled, and held out her hand to him. He was powerless to deny her. She was shaking off the aftereffects that Hell and Vega had left on her and was shining bright again. He grasped her hand and kissed her before he switched his attention to Nora who grabbed his shirt with a tiny fist and stared at him with impatient eyes.

"Dada!"

He couldn't stop his shit-eating grin. He was never going to tire of hearing his title. Nora chanted it daily, and it was music to his ears. He couldn't be more delighted that dada had been her first word. He settled Nora in the crook of his arm while Lyla introduced Isabel's fiancé, Marv, and his daughter, Maddie.

"Cousin," Angel said as he kissed Lyla on the cheek.

He draped an arm over her shoulder and whispered something that caused her to give him a dirty look. Angel grinned and said something else that made her laugh and shake her head. When she wrapped an arm around his waist and leaned into him, he saw Angel fully relax. Lyla's light had the same calming effect on Angel that it did on him. Angel didn't have his family to keep him anchored, so they needed to step in. When they returned from Bora Bora, he would make a point to have his cousin come by more often. Angel treated Lyla with the same warm affection he had for Luci. The Romans had accepted her as one of their own. He'd heard Lyla on the phone with Luci several times. He didn't know what was said, but the contentment Lyla exuded afterward boded well.

He wasn't pleased when Blade came up beside him since Nora reached for him. Blade took the baby who rested her cheek on his chest and sucked her thumb. Carmen arrived, dressed as if she was on her way to the opera. He knew she was behind this get-together, but he couldn't find it in him to be pissed when everyone was having a good time. They settled around the table as the food was served, women on one side with the men on the other. It took him less than five minutes to discern that Marv Armstrong was a good man. Blade and Angel were impressed with Marv. He served in the military, ran his own mechanic shop, and loved to hunt.

He was glad when the evening wore down, and they escorted people to the door.

"Thank you for coming," Lyla said as she hugged and kissed Isabel.

He shook hands with Marv and nodded at Maddie. She met his gaze for a moment before she flushed and looked away. Lyla waved them off before she turned to him with a dazzling smile.

"You had fun, didn't you?"

He shrugged and pulled her into the house so he could kick the door shut. He was very aware of the staff still in the kitchen and the fact they still had some guests in the house, but he was distracted by her warm weight against him. When she pulled him toward the couch, he didn't fight. She pushed him down on the cushions and then curled into his side.

"I had a great day." She sighed. "Hair and shopping with Carmen and then a great dinner with friends and family."

He slipped his hands through her blond locks. "I'm glad you didn't cut or dye it."

"Of course, you are."

"You're always messing with me." She had been teasing him for days, threatening to dye it some ugly ass color.

"You're so easy," she said lazily.

He loved her hair, and she knew it. It was shiny and heavy, and he loved falling asleep with it tangled around him or wrapping his fist in spun gold as he fucked her.

"Two more days until Bora Bora," she said.

"Yes."

"Are you excited?"

"I'm looking forward to it."

His life revolved around Las Vegas. Between the casinos and the underworld, he had no reason to leave the city. The longest he had ever been absent was when he served time in prison. But times had changed. He wasn't the crime lord any longer, and he had a COO who could run the casinos all by himself. Marcus and Angel had given him more leeway than he ever had. In his twenties, he thought money and power gave him freedom, but he was wrong. It was a ball and chain that nearly destroyed everyone around him.

He had been arrogant and foolish in his youth. He thought he was indestructible and could rule the underworld without paying his dues. Vinny's and his father's deaths changed him. Life was so fucking short, and he was glad Lyla gave her ultimatum. It forced him to look beyond the underworld to something worth fighting for. He would ensure Angel's reign as long as he wanted it, and in the meantime, he would fulfill his promise to Lyla and give her the paradise she deserved.

He played with the ends of her hair as they sat in silence, their feet side by side on the coffee table. For the first time in his life, everything was in its place. He didn't feel the hunger that drove Marcus in business or Angel in the underworld. He had exceeded every goal he set for himself. There were no more mountains to climb, no one to kill. The unquenchable need to conquer was now focused on Lyla.

His hand moved over her stomach. "Have you taken a pregnancy test?"

The loss of his father and Vinny left a chasm inside him that hungered for what only she could give him. He needed more. Nora was the best thing that ever happened to him. Every day she grew stronger. He saw a glimmer of the woman she'd become. He couldn't wait for her to learn to talk in complete sentences and grow into her personality. She was the perfect mix of him and Lyla, a part of them that would live past their time. One day, they wouldn't be here, and Nora needed siblings for permanent backup. He wanted to see what their kids looked like, and if they'd all have Lyla's stunning eyes. He wanted to see their similarities and differences and wanted the challenge of being the father to a huge brood.

Vinny's loss haunted him. He saw it still had a hold on Carmen as well. She was pushing hard for the same reasons he was—they fucking owed it to Vinny and his father to live life to the fullest so their deaths wouldn't be in vain. He had Lyla and Nora, and he was going to give them all he had.

"I'm not pregnant," Lyla said.

"How do you know?"

"I just do."

He rubbed her stomach. "I'm surprised you haven't gotten pregnant." He'd been trying his damndest.

"Gavin, it's only been four months."

Yeah, four months of constant fucking. Maybe he needed to put more time into the project.

The front door opened. He turned his head to see who the fuck was coming in when everyone was supposed to get *out*. His COO walked in and spotted them.

"Marcus!" Lyla exclaimed and rose to hug him.

Marcus grinned as he engulfed her in his arms. "How are you doing?"

"I'm excellent. I wish you could have come earlier. I set aside some food for you just in case."

"Sorry I missed the party. Is Carmen still here?" Marcus asked.

"Yes, she's out back."

"Are you excited about your trip?"

Lyla beamed. "Yes! Maybe you can take Carmen somewhere once we get back."

Marcus glanced at him before he murmured, "Maybe."

"You can," Gavin said.

Carmen said something to that effect earlier. If Marcus wanted time off, he hadn't said a damn thing. Marcus wasn't shy. He was always pushing him to expand, rebrand, or renovate something. Marcus was right where he wanted to be. It was Carmen who wanted to go off wherever the fuck she wanted to and force Marcus along. He didn't approve of their fuck buddy relationship. Carmen was hell on wheels, and there was no controlling her. She would go where the wind blew her and get into any activity that had some amount of danger and risk involved. She was reckless and insane. He watched his cousin chase after her for most of their relationship. Marcus was no match for her.

"Where's my goddaughter?" Marcus asked.

"Blade put her to sleep."

"I'll have to stop by to see her when you two get back." He tilted his head to the side as he surveyed Lyla. "You're glowing."

Gavin yanked Lyla down on the couch beside him. "Fuck off, Marcus."

He didn't like any man close to Lyla, even if it was Marcus. His COO wasn't offended. Marcus tipped his head back and laughed uproariously while Lyla shot him a reproachful look. He wasn't in the mood for Marcus' antics when he was thinking about getting her pregnant.

"I better fetch Carmen before he goes postal," Marcus said to Lyla before he headed toward the back of the house.

Lyla smacked his chest. "What the hell is wrong with you?"

"What?"

"You are so weird. You work with Marcus every day and still act like he's a threat."

"I don't want his scent on you."

"What?"

"I don't want to smell another man's cologne on you when I fuck you."

She collapsed against him with a groan. "You're crazy."

"And you love it."

He saw her mouth curve as she murmured, "I guess I do."

Several minutes later, Carmen rushed by and said something he didn't bother to pay attention to as she left with Marcus in tow. Angel followed several minutes later.

"Have a safe trip and don't worry about anything," Angel said as he kissed Lyla's cheek.

Gavin glanced at his expression and knew he was going hunting. "Watch your back."

Angel nodded. When the last of the staff shuffled out the door, he finally relaxed.

"I'm going out," Blade said.

Lyla whipped around and propped her elbows on the back of the couch. "You need to get laid again?"

Blade didn't answer. He walked out and slammed the door.

He tapped Lyla's ass. "Why do you want to know if he's getting laid?"

"Because!"

"Because why?"

She frowned. "Why doesn't he talk to me about it?"

"About getting laid? Why the fuck do you need to know that?"

She waved her hands. "I don't want to know *that*. It's just … he doesn't even talk to me."

"He does."

"No, he doesn't. He just grunts and tells me what to do. He doesn't talk about himself."

"He doesn't want to."

"Why?"

"Not everyone has a past they want to talk about." In fact, none of them did. Marcus, Blade, Angel, himself. All of their pasts were twisted and fucked up. Why would they share it with anyone, especially someone who couldn't relate? "Leave him be. He's fine."

"But—"

He dragged her onto his lap. "I don't think Blade should be the only one getting laid tonight."

She smiled, and it made strange things happen in his chest. A part of him hated it, that a mere smile from her could make his heart change its rhythm, but he had finally accepted it. The only alternative was not having her at all, and that would never happen. She framed his face with her tiny hands and kissed him. She was in the mood. She was kissing him hard and rubbing her pussy against his already hard dick. He gripped her ass and ground her against him. She lifted her head and looked down at him.

"You think this will ever fade?" she asked.

"No."

There was no doubt in his mind that he would always be desperate for her. His father never got over his mom, and he was going to be the same way. Even when he was eighty, he would be going down on Lyla in a fucking closet while their grandkids opened presents around the tree.

She kissed the corner of his mouth. When he tried to capture her lips, she kissed his jaw and then nipped his earlobe.

"I want to go down on you."

His fingers bit into her ass.

"I've been thinking about it all night."

He yanked on her hair so he could see her face. The lust in her eyes made his muscles lock with anticipation.

"You've been thinking about sucking me off with friends and family around?"

"You're a bad influence."

Fuck yeah, he was. "Show me what you've been thinking about."

She kissed his neck while she undid his buttons. She sucked lightly before she used her teeth.

"Gavin."

He realized he had her locked against him and forced himself to let go. She slipped down his body and left a trail of wet down his abdomen before she landed at his feet. Her blue eyes hypnotized him as she knelt between his spread thighs.

"What?" he bit out.

She grinned and shook her head. "Nothing."

When she stroked the inside of his thighs, his hands curled into fists to stop himself from reaching for her. When she pulled down his zipper, his cock was standing at attention. She rested her head against his thigh and extended her tongue to lap at the base. He glared at her as she smiled at him and continued feathering her tongue around his dick when she knew what he really wanted.

"I'm going to come on your face," he threatened.

Her voice was supremely unconcerned as she said, "Fine with me."

He was seconds away from shoving her on her back and fucking her mouth when her lips closed around his head. She stroked down firmly, making his eyes roll. *Holy fuck.* He'd taught her exactly what he wanted. She knew exactly how much pressure to use, what he wanted her hands and tongue to do simultaneously, and to keep eye contact the whole time. The blue diamond on her ring flashed as it stroked his cock. The sight of his brand on her finger satisfied him immensely. Anything he could put on her to declare to the world that she was his, he would do. Lyla's hair brushed over his sensitive skin, and the hum she let out while she sucked made him jerk.

"Lyla, fuck. I'm not going to last."

"Give it to me," she said around his cock.

"I want to come inside you."

"Come in my mouth," she breathed as she followed a thick vein on the top of his dick with her tongue.

He tried to draw her up his body, but she wouldn't budge. She grabbed his cock with two hands, one at the base and the other stroking while her mouth did wicked things to his balls. He couldn't take it. He grabbed her head and shoved in, going as deep as he could go before coming in her mouth.

"Oh, fuck," he groaned.

When he slumped against the couch, Lyla cleaned him up before she rose. He watched with lazy eyes as she slipped out of her dress. When she climbed on the couch and put her glistening pussy in front of him, he didn't hesitate. He cupped her ass and drew her against his mouth. Her hands yanked at his hair while she rubbed herself over his face. When he slipped his fingers in her, she tossed her head back and moaned. Eating her out was one of his favorite pastimes. It didn't take long for her to start humping his face. When she climaxed, she reared backward. He caught her and dropped her on the couch and finished her while she trembled beneath him and then pushed his head away.

"Too much," she moaned.

He chuckled as he rose and draped her over his shoulder while she was still shaking with the aftershocks. She grumbled under her breath about how he was supposed to give her piggybacks. He ignored her as he climbed the stairs and set her on her feet in the shower. She leaned against him, telling him without words to take over.

He liked her sated and lazy. She held his waist while he soaped her up and then bundled her into a robe. She was struggling to stay awake when he placed her in bed.

He checked on Nora who was sound asleep. He slipped his hand through her unruly curls and grinned when she tried to smack his hand away. So small and defiant, just like her mother. Carmen thought he was getting his just deserts by having a demanding and wild daughter. He wouldn't want it any other way.

He glanced at the dogs curled up together a few feet from the crib. Honey thumped her tail when he looked at her, and he shook his head. The dog's instincts were definitely off. When he walked back into their room, Lyla was buried beneath the duvet with only her hair showing. He sat up in bed with his laptop and clicked through some emails. Fucking Marcus, he didn't know when to quit. He was a ruthless bastard in business. He was making him more money than ever before, but it also required more fucking attention.

An hour later, he received a notification letting him know that Blade returned. He dismissed it, shut down the laptop, and drew Lyla against his chest. He slipped his hand beneath the robe and gripped her breast. Her rough, raised scars rubbed against his skin, a reminder that it was a fucking miracle she was here. He buried his face in her hair and drew in her scent.

He wasn't sure when he drifted off, but he woke to the sound of her ragged breathing. Lyla was trembling like a plucked string. He turned on a light and saw that she was covered in sweat. Her brows were drawn together, and her hands rose, reaching for something.

"Lyla."

Her eyes opened halfway, showing only white and no

hint of blue. He shook her and got more than he bargained for when she swung a balled fist, clipping him on the jaw. He cursed and pinned her arms over her head. She fought him for all she was worth, body bowing, limbs thrashing.

"Lyla!"

One sweaty hand slipped out of his. Her nails came right for his eyes. He deflected but not quickly enough. She raked her nails down his cheek. The burn roused his beast. He gave her a rough shake, which slammed her teeth together. Her eyes finally opened, but there was no recognition, only bloodlust.

"Lyla, wake the fuck up."

She bared her teeth at him and let out a bloodcurdling scream that raised the hair on the nape of his neck. It was a war cry filled with fury and pain. Before she finished, Nora's piercing cry split the air. Lyla went silent and blinked rapidly, her maternal instinct overcoming her nightmare. Her dilated pupils finally focused on him. She trembled uncontrollably, face ghost white.

"You with me?" he asked.

Her eyes closed, but not before he saw the glimmer of wet. She covered her face with shaking hands.

"I'm sorry," she whispered.

"It's just a dream." He wanted to comfort her, but Nora was screaming at the top of her lungs.

"Could you see to her? I-I can't ..."

"I'll be back."

He rolled out of bed and stepped into the hallway. Out of the corner of his eye, he saw Blade clear the stairs and head in his direction. He entered the nursery, pulled Nora out of the crib, and tucked the baby under his chin while her tiny tears hit his chest.

Blade stopped a few feet away. His eyes touched on

Gavin's cheek before it went across the hall to the master suite.

"You heard her?" Gavin asked.

Blade held up his wrist, showing his watch, which vibrated if there were any spikes in Lyla's heart monitor. Blade should have disabled it since Gavin was home, but he wasn't surprised that he hadn't. Blade never let down his guard and was bonded to Lyla and Nora in a way Gavin never expected when he appointed him as Lyla's bodyguard.

"She okay?" Blade asked.

He nuzzled Nora who hiccupped against his chest. "It was a bad one."

"No shit." Blade held his hands out for Nora. "I'll take care of her. See to Lyla."

He handed the baby to Blade and was mildly peeved when Nora instantly quieted at Blade's stern, "Hush." He entered their room and stopped when he saw the empty bed. His adrenaline spiked.

"Lyla!"

No answer. She wouldn't ... He was about to run out of the room to search the house when he registered the faint sound coming from the dark bathroom. He slammed his hand on the light switch and saw Lyla in the shower, one hand braced against the wall, head bowed as the water beat down on her. *Fuck*. She was gonna give him a fucking heart attack.

He opened the door and was engulfed in steam. "What the fuck was that?"

She didn't acknowledge him.

"Lyla," he bit out.

When he reached for her, she evaded his hand.

"Don't touch me," she said hoarsely.

His beast slipped the leash, and he let it. He turned off

the water. She further incited his beast when she slapped his hand as it closed around her upper arm.

"What the hell are you doing?" she shouted.

He dragged her out of the bathroom and tossed her on the bed. He didn't care that she was dripping wet or still shaken from her dream. When she tried to roll away, he grabbed her ankle and yanked her to the edge of the bed. Her other foot lashed out and caught him on the shoulder with enough force to make him stagger back two steps. His beast growled in approval, but Gavin wasn't amused. He was fucking pissed. She was on her way to the closet when he grabbed her hair and yanked her backward. He banded an arm around her waist when she collided against him.

"Don't you fucking walk away from me," he hissed.

"You need to let me go."

Her voice was nowhere near cowed.

"How many times have you asked me to do that?" he hissed in her ear.

"This time, you need to do it," she said before she stomped his bare foot with her heel.

Game fucking over. He shoved her down on her hands and knees and pinned her with a hand at the top of her spine. His palm landed on her wet ass. The force of the blow mashed her face into the carpet. She screamed, but it wasn't from pain. It was fury. Good. Now they were even. He walloped her ass. The sharp sound of his hand hitting her flesh and the sting and tingle in his hand alleviated the pounding in his head. Her muffled threats and curses spurred him on. When his hand was throbbing and her ass was bright red, he stopped. Immediately, she tried to rolled away. He stopped her when she was flat on her back with a hand on her throat and crouched over her.

"Who's the fucking boss?"

Her eyes glittered with rage. "Fuck you!"

"Wrong answer, baby girl."

He put his legs on either side of hers and pulled his rock-hard cock out of his pants. He saw her hands coming toward his face again and pinned them over her head. He pressed the head of his cock against her opening.

"What the fuck is wrong with you?" she shouted.

"Don't tell me not to touch you." A few choice words from her could send him off the deep end. The need to have her submit to him made his cock throb with the need to invade the pussy that was made for him. "You don't pull away from me."

"I didn't!"

"You fucking did."

"The dream—"

He didn't want to hear what she had to say. He forced the head of his cock in. She was barely wet enough to take him, and her hiss of pain was music to his ears. He kept her thighs clamped together, creating an even tighter channel. His beast salivated as it looked over his meal. Her squeaky-clean skin begged him to cover her with cum. Lyla roused every primitive instinct he possessed and had the complete attention of his beast, which didn't fuck around, especially when it came to its mate.

Tears shimmered in her eyes like unshed diamonds. "This isn't about you, Gavin."

"Then why am I bleeding?" He pushed through her folds, forcing her pussy to take him. "You're pulling away from me because of some dead phantom. I won't allow it. They're not here. I am." He pulled out and then slammed back in, which made her grit her teeth against the pain.

"They're not allowed in my bed or in our relationship.

You need to know exactly where you are and who you belong to."

"I know who I belong to," she said through clenched teeth.

"Then say it."

She glared at him mutinously. He wouldn't accept half measures from her. He rode her hard, never breaking eye contact with that feral silver blue gaze. His wife wanted to challenge him. He didn't mind as long as she could take the heat. Battling with her fed his darker needs.

Despite his superior strength and knowledge of combat, she still put up a fight. He liked the tears and even her anger. He would take anything over the inanimate doll she became when she allowed the past into her head. He wouldn't allow it. Vega was dead, and they were moving on. He wouldn't let her wallow in the past.

"You're heartless," she said raggedly.

"I'm keeping you with me."

"I am with you."

"No, you aren't." He pressed his forehead against hers, and when she tried to turn her face away, he grabbed it and turned it back to him. She fought him, but he held her down, bruising her in his quest to keep her right where he wanted her. He was jealous of those who haunted her nightmares. She was his, no one else's, and certainly not Steven Vega's. He was nothing, a pissant, a coward. He was ash now, and that was all that mattered.

"You have no one to fear," he said as he thrust hard enough to make her gasp. "You don't belong to them; you belong to me."

"I know that!"

"Then look at me. Feel me. You feel that cock stretching you? That's throbbing for you? That's all that matters."

He wasn't deep enough. He jerked out and flipped her onto her stomach and positioned her on her hands and knees. He forced her head down, gripped her hips, and let his beast reign. He pounded her tender ass. She screamed, and he gloried in it. It fed his bloodlust. The only one she needed to fear was him.

When she was raw and pleading, he turned her over and slipped back into her. She stared up at him, face streaked with tears. He gripped her face as he drove his aching cock into her.

"Do you understand?" he hissed.

She nodded.

"They don't get to take you from me. Not a minute, not even in your fucking dreams. Every time they intrude, I'm bringing you back any way I see fit. You understand?"

Her breath hitched, and she reached between them and gripped his cock, which jerked.

"Make me forget, Gavin."

He fucked her hard and smothered her face when she screamed. When he came inside her, his vision flashed white. He collapsed on top of her and tried to catch his breath. When he gathered the strength to move, he peeled their sweaty skin apart and found that she was passed out beneath him.

He was such a good husband. He fucked the nightmares right out of his wife. He checked her to make sure he hadn't done too much damage, then went into the bathroom to clean himself. Leaning toward the mirror, he examined the scratches on his face, which were seeping blood. His wife was a wild one. He brought back a washcloth to wipe his dripping seed. No blood. She didn't stir, which pleased him. This is how his wife should be—so worn out from fucking that she slept peacefully.

He examined her ass, which was red and showed the promise of bruising. He placed her in bed and brushed her damp hair from her face. Lyla was his sleeping beauty— gold hair, blue eyes, and oh so innocent before he entered her life. She let the big bad wolf get her and even came with a wicked father who wanted to do her harm.

Lyla was a far cry from the innocent who offered him her virginity. Being in his world changed her and tailored her into the woman he needed—a woman who would stand beside him and protect what was theirs. He approved of her bite. His eyes lingered over the faint tear trails on her cheeks. He wouldn't allow her dreams of phantoms and other dead people to affect her thoughts and feelings. There was enough to keep her occupied in the present. Besides, only he was allowed to make her cry.

He kissed her pouty lips and skimmed his fingertips over her skin while she lay pliant and still in his arms. He traced the scars on her chest over and over, as he had on so many other nights. Wrath burned in his gut. He allowed the fire to course through his veins. He may not be the crime lord any longer, but he would make sure to keep his edge. There was bound to be some idiot who wanted to challenge him. He would hit back so hard no one would dare touch what was his.

Just before sunrise, Lyla let out a whimper. He looked down and saw her features screwed up in acute mental anguish. He tipped her on her back and spread her legs. He pressed against her opening and eased the head in. She went rigid and tried to get away, but he kept her where he wanted her, taking his cock.

"You feel me, baby?" he murmured. "I'm the baddest motherfucker in the city. I'm the only one you need to worry about. Tell them fuck off and come play with me."

Lyla frowned, still locked in her bad dream. Her hands plucked at the sheets and her legs jerked, but she wasn't coordinated enough to put up a fight. Good. He didn't want to tussle so early in the morning. He was in the mood to savor. He watched her face as he eased in and out of her pussy. She looked confused as hell, which made him grin.

"I like seeing you helpless," he murmured in her ear. "Even in sleep, you respond to me. You're getting wet. Such a good girl. You know daddy's voice, hmm?"

She gave him another whimper, but she wasn't near tears anymore. She was still locked in sleep while he played her body.

"You sore, baby? Is that why you're squeezing me so tight?" He licked her ear and then bit down. "Good. You're gonna think of me every time you try to sit or bend over today."

Her face screwed up again, and her hands twitched at her sides. Even as he rocked in and out of her, a tear slid out of the corner of her eye.

"I dream of your dad too, but in it, I'm slitting his throat," he confessed as he licked away the tear and peppered kisses over her face when her breathing hitched in distress. "You're safe with me ... for the moment."

He stroked her rounded stomach. She wasn't as thin as she had been before Nora. The pregnancy weight turned into muscle, which she had begun to use against him. It fired up his blood. His wife was being trained into a warrior and had no qualms about using her newfound knowledge and strength against him. He loved it.

"I'll train you so you can last longer than a few minutes when we spar. Maybe I'll get you pregnant when I have you bound and gagged in the basement." The memory of the last time they fucked in the basement made him groan. "I better fuck you raw now. Can't fuck you too rough when you're pregnant."

He stopped so he wouldn't blow. It was amazing how, even unconscious, she threatened his control. This small woman affected him on every level. She held all the fucking cards.

"You make me feel too much. You hold my reins, baby girl. Give me a lead and I'll destroy whoever you want me to."

Lyla was completely relaxed now, her nightmare gone. Her thighs were spread on either side of him. He sank into her and grinned when her eyelids fluttered, almost as if she wanted to wake but couldn't.

"Such a sound sleeper," he crooned. "The first time you came back to me I fucked you sleeping because you made this sound ..." He had to make a concentrated effort to stop his climax. "I couldn't wait. You knew me even in sleep, just as I'd know you. We haven't even skimmed the surface of what we can be together."

He sat up and positioned her thighs so he could go even deeper. Her calves flexed, and she arched as her head tossed restlessly on the pillow.

"Will you give me a son next, baby girl?" He couldn't go slow any longer. He pumped into her and held her down with a hand on her chest to stop her from turning on her side. "I love seeing you pregnant and having everyone know who owns you. You'll give me warriors. You'll give me every-thing I ask because I won't accept anything less."

Her breasts moved in rhythm with his thrusts. He willed her eyes to open so he could see them glazed with lust or shock or pleasure, but they remained closed. Her breathing was uneven and her hands gripped the pillow while beads of perspiration dotted her forehead.

He gripped her hips and punched deep. She let out a choked scream, hands flailing and hitting his chest while he groaned and filled her. He nuzzled her cheek while his cock wept happily inside her.

He kissed her cheek as she settled beneath him. "Don't challenge me unless you want to pay the consequences."

6

Lyla woke spread eagled in bed with a cold, wet spot under her ass and a familiar stickiness between her legs. "Fucking Gavin."

She grit her teeth as she sat up. That fucker went to town on her last night. She hobbled into the bathroom and examined her bruised rump before she stepped in the shower. She had just finished blow-drying her hair when Gavin walked in. He wore a white button up tucked into navy slacks. His eyes were a shade lighter than usual, which told her his beast was still at the forefront. She eyed him balefully as he came up behind her and gripped the vanity on either side of her.

"Sore?"

"What do you think?"

"I think you deserved it."

She whirled in the circle of his arms. The scratches on his cheek were noticeable, but just barely. It was typical that the scratches didn't ruin his sex appeal. He wore battle wounds the same way he wore everything—with effortless arrogance. "I clawed you *in my sleep,* and I get a bruised ass?"

"You threw down."

"I was having a nightmare. I didn't know what I was doing."

He lifted the back of her robe and examined her ass in the mirror. He didn't look the least bit contrite. On the contrary, he looked pleased. "I can handle being scratched by a kitty. I don't mind the tap on the chin you gave me either." His fingers skimmed her swollen rump, and she tensed, waiting for another teeth-jarring smack. "It's what you did after that set me off."

"After?"

"You pulled away from me. You told me not to touch you."

"When I relive that shit, I need a moment, Gavin! You're always coming at me. You don't let me *breathe*!"

He ignored her statement by pressing her tender ass against the vanity. When she made a bid for space, he pinned her hands behind her back and forced her chest against his. *Seriously?* She had one really bad nightmare, and he went fucking psycho alpha on her.

"You don't need time to think or breathe in that shit. You need to stay in the present with me. They're dead, Lyla."

"I know they are," she said through clenched teeth. "I can't control my dreams."

"You have a guilty conscience."

"I don't."

"Then what was it about? Steven? Your father?" He cocked his head when she didn't speak. "My father?"

Her heart wriggled uncomfortably. "It doesn't matter now, does it?"

He cupped her chin. "Was it Dad?"

She swallowed hard. "I don't want to talk about it."

His thumb glided over her bottom lip. "Don't let the past overshadow the present. We're still here."

Her eyes filled with tears. "I know."

"We've been through too much to let any of that hold us back. You don't pull away from me. I won't tolerate it."

"I noticed," she muttered and searched his face. "You don't ever dream about ... anything?"

"Rarely and when I do, it's satisfying. I'm the one doing the killing."

"I'm not like you," she said quietly.

"I know." He released her and kissed her forehead. "I love you."

"I know."

Hazel eyes bored into hers. "Say it back."

"I love you, *boss*."

He relaxed instantly. "That's what I want to hear. Do you want me to stay home?"

Gavin Pyre was hot, cold, sweet, and brutal wrapped up into one confounding male. He beat her ass for something she couldn't control and then asked her if she wanted him to stay home.

"Go to work." It was going to be damn uncomfortable today, but she could handle it. She didn't need him in her face. "I have stuff to do."

He gave her a soft pat on the butt. "It's been a while since you got a spanking."

"That hurts, you ass!"

He gave her a wolfish grin. "That's the point. You'll be feeling me all day."

"And how about in two days when we're on the damn plane?"

"You'll be fine by then."

"How the hell do you know?"

"Not my first rodeo."

She grabbed her perfume bottle and threw it at him. He laughed as he backed toward the exit.

"Why do you think I went easy on you?"

"Easy on me?" she shouted, but he was already gone. "Motherfucker."

She surveyed her wardrobe. There was no way in hell she was going to wear jeans ... or bottoms at all, for that matter. She eyed the dresses she bought for her tropical vacation. The light fabric would be her best friend today. She slipped into a fiery maxi dress with a halter neckline that covered her chest but had an open, sultry back. She secured the top with a bow on the back of her neck. She grabbed a jean jacket just in case and finished the outfit with fancy flip-flops.

When she entered the kitchen, she found Nora in a high chair with Blade eating oatmeal at the table. The dogs greeted her before they flopped on the floor. Lyla pressed kisses over her daughter's animated face. The nightmare had been a new, terrifying one. It featured her in the pit with Steven, her father, and a bunch of men in white masks coming at her with weapons. She was holding Nora in the crook of her arm, and Manny was taking his last breaths at her feet. The arena was filled with the roar of the blood-thirsty crowd, and she had no help. She did the unthinkable, and even as she did it in the dream, Gavin was shaking her awake, which caused her to lash out. She'd slit her daughter's throat so they wouldn't torture her or force her to watch. What kind of mother even dreamed of such a thing?

She cupped Nora's face with a shaking hand. "You're safe." It was just a dream.

When she looked up, Blade jerked his chin. She followed his silent direction and saw the painkillers waiting for her. She gave him a haughty look even as she reached for them. Gavin wouldn't tell him, would he? She didn't want to think about it. She fixed herself a bowl of oatmeal and decided to eat standing. Blade ignored her as he flipped through the newspaper. He had been giving her the cold shoulder since she suggested he take some time off while they went to Bora Bora. He was insulted when he should have been grateful.

"Anything interesting?" she asked.

He shook his head.

Mr. Communicative. "Are you ready for the trip?"

He grunted as he skimmed an article.

"Are the dogs fed?" He didn't bother to answer since the dog bowls had been licked clean. Determined to get a reaction she asked, "How was your fuck last night?"

Blade eyed her reproachfully and flicked his eyes at Nora.

"Blade, she's seven months."

He went back to the newspaper. Blade worried about her language. She'd have to tell Carmen that one. Blade acted menacing and detached, but he was as sunk for Nora as Gavin. They were two warriors who managed to rein it in for a tiny baby. She couldn't believe it. Blade had better luck keeping Nora quiet than she did. Even now, Nora sat in the high chair, playing with a bright hammer that would play snippets of sound whenever she hit something. How Blade could read with that racket was a mystery.

"Did you stay with your booty call all night?" His black eyes flicked to her, telling her without words that he didn't want to discuss this, but she needed a distraction, and he was the only one here. "Do you go to a strip club to pick someone?"

He folded the paper and picked up his bowl.

"Come on, Blade."

"Gavin said no training." Blade soaked his bowl in the sink and then turned to her. "And I didn't stay out all night. My watch went off during your nightmare, and I took Nora downstairs while Gavin disciplined you."

She flushed with mortification. Blade sure knew how to put her in her place.

"From the looks of it, he took it easy on you."

She gaped. "Are you fucking serious?"

His eyes flicked to Nora again, and this time, he actually looked upset. "Watch it."

"You think he took it easy on me? I won't be able to sit down for days!"

"At least you can stand."

She stared at him. "Seriously?"

He shrugged. "You marked him."

She stomped her foot. "A tiny *scratch!*"

"Gavin's on a hair trigger, and he doesn't have another outlet."

"And I'm supposed to be the punching bag?"

"You can channel his energy any way you choose. I'd say from his mood this morning, he enjoyed it, so keep doing whatever you want, just be prepared for consequences."

"You guys are messed up." Blade was like a fucked-up Yoda, giving her advice to tame Gavin.

"You're dressed to go out," he said, ignoring her outrage.

"I'm taking the dogs to Aunt Isabel's."

He glanced at his watch. "Departure time about an hour from now?"

"Yes."

He reached for his phone and began to make some calls. Blade and Gavin weren't taking any chances. She had an escort of ten to twenty guards whether she was going to the salon or her aunt's house. The security detail would meet to discuss the route and have an emergency plan in place before they left.

Blade wandered out of the room, leaving her with Nora. She went to the baby and ran her finger along her daughter's tiny neck and shivered. Killing her father and Steven in cold blood changed her. She didn't think the same, and her moral compass hadn't found a true North yet. There was a darkness inside her that she couldn't purge. Now she knew what she was capable of. She would maim, murder, and torture to protect or avenge. What kind of mother was she? At times, she wanted to confide in Gavin, Blade, or Carmen about her dreams, fears, and sanity, but she already knew what they would say. Either they would placate her and say it would pass, or tell her they had the same dark thoughts. She wasn't sure which was worse.

Nora reached for her. She hesitated before she picked up her child. She held Nora close and breathed in her scent. She would protect Nora even from herself.

An hour later, they piled into an SUV with Blade riding shotgun and the dogs, Nora, and herself in the back. Three SUVs accompanied them to Aunt Isabel's new home that she shared with her fiancé. They pulled up to a picturesque house with a garden, tidy lawn, and even a white picket fence. Lyla climbed out of the SUV and paused to take it in while she held Nora on her hip. She had a moment of deja vu even though she had never been here before. This house was what she had pictured for herself. A simple home and the love of a kind man. It was a dream that would never be fulfilled.

"Dada," Nora said, reminding Lyla of the irrevocable path she was already on.

She pressed her forehead against Nora's. "I know, baby."

Aunt Isabel opened the front door and waved. "Come in!"

Blade let the dogs out, and they bolted for her aunt. She walked up to the door, flanked by security. She had to nudge her guards out of the way so she could hug her.

"Last night was wonderful," Aunt Isabel said warmly as she took Nora who kicked her legs excitedly.

"I'm glad you enjoyed yourself." She smiled at Marv and held out her hand. Like last night, he wrapped her in a tight hug as if they'd known each other for years.

"Nice to see you again, darling," he said.

She was embarrassed by the prick of tears. As soon as he let go, she moved away to hide her reaction. Being around another father figure who treated her with kindness and care was overwhelming when she was still raw from her father's betrayal. After being duped by Steven, her walls were sky high, but Marv ... He was good people. So was his daughter, Maddie, who she'd taken a liking to. Maddie was young and sweet. She reminded her of the innocent she had been before the Pyres entered her life.

"So when's the big day?" she asked Aunt Isabel.

"We're holding off until Marv's son can come home from Japan. His wife is too far along in her pregnancy to travel."

"Oh! Is this your first grandchild?" she asked Marv.

He puffed out his chest. "Yes. I can't wait to see him."

She tried to smile but wasn't sure she succeeded. Marv was clearly excited for his first grandchild and was even postponing his wedding so the whole family could be there while her father tried to kill his and Beatrice refused to see Nora.

Determined not to be a fucking rain cloud, she went to the living area and was about to sit when her ass protested. Fucking Gavin.

"Where are you having the wedding?" she asked.

"Come, let me show you." Aunt Isabel linked their arms together and led her into the backyard. "Isn't it perfect?"

It was. Beau and Honey ran beneath the shade of some trees that had to be over fifty years old. The yard was well tended with mature plants and a riot of colorful flowers. There was a white bench placed between two trees and a stone path that wove through a small Japanese garden.

"It's beautiful," she said quietly.

Aunt Isabel rested her head on her shoulder. "Isn't it?"

"I'm so happy for you, Aunty."

Aunt Isabel straightened and looked at her with maternal concern. "And you, Lyla? Are you happy?"

The dent Marv put in her shield became a hole. Her emotions escaped, which caused her eyes to fill.

"I'm happy," she said in a trembling voice.

"Aw, honey." Aunt Isabel pressed their cheeks together and cupped the back of her head. "I try to see your mother every week. It's so hard to see her that way. I know you blame yourself, but you can't."

She closed her eyes and let out a shuddering breath.

"You have a beautiful baby and a husband who loves you. You can't control what happens with your mom, but you have us."

Lyla hugged her tight. "I know. Thank you." She wanted to say more, but she couldn't without losing it completely.

Aunt Isabel pulled back and brushed a hand down her face. "You and Carmen have been through so much. I can see the sadness in your eyes. You're trying so hard to be happy. You'll get there. It takes time."

"I know. I have good and bad days."

Aunt Isabel nodded wisely. "It may always be like that. Don't worry about the dogs. We'll take good care of them.

They're going to have a blast at Marv's Utah cabin. They'll get fresh air and get to mark all the trees."

Lyla laughed. "Yes, they'll enjoy that." She hesitated and then asked, "Can I leave Nora with you for a little bit? I think I'll visit my mom before I go on this trip."

"Of course, dear."

When she walked back in the house, she found Marv and Blade standing over Nora who was crawling around the living room, investigating her brand-new surroundings. Blade's black gaze settled on her face and sharpened.

"I'm going to visit Mom and leave Nora here," she said to Blade.

He nodded and spoke quickly to the men. They left a host of men to guard Nora while the others accompanied her. The trip to her mom's house didn't take long. Aunt Isabel helped them find a place near her and agreed to assist Beatrice as much as possible.

Her mother's house was in a safe neighborhood. Lyla briefly considered getting her mom a condo, but in the end, she decided that a private outdoor space would be a great haven for her mom as she healed mentally, spiritually, and physically. She did a walk-through of the house before her mom moved in but hadn't been back since.

The house was a one-story cottage painted a soft white. There was a tiny yard with a tree in front. Blade walked her to the door while four men brought up the back. She hadn't brought her gun. After a nightmare like the one she had last night, she remained on edge for days after and became prone to panic attacks and even hallucinations. She didn't allow herself to carry a weapon unless she was rock steady.

A nurse opened the door. She looked alarmed by the crowd until she spotted Lyla.

"Hi, Mrs. Pyre."

Lyla entered the house, which was done in a very pale shade of peach, her mom's favorite color. "How is she?"

The nurse's eyes flicked from her to the guards before she said, "She hasn't been eating ..."

Lyla's stomach clenched. "Can I see her?"

"Sure."

Lyla indicated Blade should stay in the living room. She walked down the short hallway and sighed when she felt his massive bulk right behind her. He rarely listened to her. The nurse opened the door of the master bedroom, which was pitch black.

"Mom?"

No answer.

The nurse turned on the light. Her mother lay on her side facing them. Beatrice didn't flinch when the light came on. Her feral gaze was focused on Lyla who resisted the urge to back away. No matter how many times she saw her mother, she would never get used to her appearance. Her mother's once attractive face was permanently disfigured. Every inch of her body was covered in deep, slashing scars. Chunks of flesh were missing from her nose, cheek, arms, and legs. Her glass eye was disconcerting and because of her head injuries, most of her head had been shaved.

"Mom?"

She forced herself to move forward.

"Mrs. Pyre," the nurse began nervously.

"I'll call you if we need you," Lyla said as she rounded the bed and drew back the curtains from the French doors to let in the sunlight. The room opened into the backyard, which had a tiny pond and garden.

"Get," Blade said shortly to the nurse who hovered by the door.

Lyla turned and found Blade eyeing her mother who lay

on her side facing him. Her mom wore sweats despite the warm weather. The back of her bald head was covered in deep, blunt grooves that continued down her neck and into her clothes. Lyla's head began to buzz with homicidal thoughts as the image of her mother strapped to a bed flashed in her mind. She blinked rapidly as if that would dispel her memories or the metallic taste that invaded her mouth. She could still feel the buck of her gun as she unloaded into her mother's rapists. Rage tripped through her veins, causing her hand to tingle and flex at her sides. Steven Vega was gone, but the devastation he left behind would never end. He'd left his mark, and she hated him for it.

"Beatrice," Blade said, forcing Lyla to focus on the present.

No word from her mother.

To give herself time to get a grip, her gaze moved over the barren room and paused on the shattered mirror on the wall. She should have seen that coming. Even she avoided mirrors, and she could hide her scars. She took a deep breath and rounded the bed until she faced her mother.

"Mom?" She waited for a word or some movement and got nothing although one blue eye was fixed on her. "The nurse says you aren't eating."

Her mom could have passed for a statue if it wasn't for that burning gaze.

"And I have reports that say you refuse to do physical therapy."

The buzzing silence was getting on her nerves, as was the way her mother was staring at her with such loathing. Their time apart hadn't improved her disposition. If anything, it seemed to have increased her hostility. If her mom had something to say, why not fucking say it?

"Is there something I can do?" she asked as she tried to read her mangled face.

"Get out."

Her mother's voice was a raspy croak. Nothing like the light, pleasing sound it had once been.

Lyla folded her arms over her chest. "I'm not leaving until you promise to eat."

Beatrice's sneer was horrifying. "You think anything you say affects me after what I've been through?"

Lyla had to make a concentrated effort to keep her expression neutral. She had given her mom the space she claimed to need, but the emaciated form beneath the sweats was unacceptable. Beatrice was wasting away, and she wouldn't allow it.

"I'm not going to let you do this to yourself."

"If you had any inkling what I went through at the hand of those monsters, you'd *leave me alone.*"

The last three words were said on a hair-raising screech. Her mother surged to a sitting position with a suddenness that belied her motionless state. Blade inserted himself between them, but Beatrice didn't even notice. Her whole focus was on Lyla. She leaned forward, deformed face terrible.

"You have no *idea* what I've been through. Every moment of every day, I'm reliving it. Drugs don't help. They even follow me in my dreams. Do you know what they did to me? Do you know what they said? How many hours I was bound while they—"

Her mother screamed and ran her nails down her cheek. Lyla leapt forward, but Blade got there first. He yanked her hands down while Beatrice bared her teeth like an animal. Blood slipped down her cheek as she stared at Lyla with a manic gaze.

"I prayed for death. I begged for it and then you come at the last second. How dare you!"

Beatrice tried to lunge, but Blade kept her on the bed. She didn't even seem to be aware of him.

"You had no right to save me. I wanted to die. I *should* have died. You think *this* is living? A life where I need help? Where no one can look at me? You think I want to live with those animals' marks all over me? Do you know how many times I was raped?"

She saw her mother's face go slack as she relived the horror. Her body began to vibrate. Beatrice pressed her face against Blade's chest and shuddered as she fought her waking nightmare. Lyla wanted to touch and soothe but knew it wouldn't be welcome and may incite her mom to violence. She watched helplessly until Beatrice lifted her face and shoved Blade away as if he was nothing. It was another indication of just how much she changed. The doctors said the trauma was bound to change her. The woman she faced today had nothing in common with the soft-spoken submissive she had been.

Beatrice jabbed a finger at her. "You bought this house because you feel guilty."

Lyla's stomach clenched.

"When your dad and I needed you, you turned from us, and now you offer help? When it's too late?"

Drool slipped out of her mouth. She wiped it away, but Lyla could see it was going to be a permanent problem because her lips didn't meet.

"You survived against all the odds. There's a reason you're still here," she whispered.

"Without your father, I have nothing."

Whatever pity she felt for her mother vanished in an instant. Her mother had Pat on a pedestal that no one could knock him off. Even in death, her mom viewed him as a fucking saint.

"You're still breathing. You have the ability to regain your strength. Some people are fighting for their lives and here you sit in a dark room, willing yourself to die."

Blade shot her a quick glance, which she ignored. It had been four months. Four months of worry, sympathy, regret, and guilt. There were things she couldn't do anything about. She couldn't change what happened at the safe house. She couldn't erase what Steven Vega did to her or the city. She couldn't will away the vicious nightmares or the panic attacks, but this—this was something they could do something about. Beatrice was still here. There could be a different outcome for her. Life was within her grasp, but she turned away from it.

"I'm not going to let you waste away."

"Watch me," Beatrice said through clenched teeth. "They raped me in front of your father. He was crying ..." Her nails curled, ready to rake down her face again, but when Blade stepped forward, she hissed at him. "They wanted something from him. He promised he would save me. He's never let me down." Beatrice ran her hands over her scarred head and then wrapped her arms around herself as she rocked. "I know this has something to do with Gavin. Pat would never get mixed up in something like that. He never would have let this happen to me."

Lyla's hands balled into fists.

"Is he really dead, or is Gavin torturing him somewhere?"

Beatrice perched on the edge of her bed, crazed eyes fixed on Lyla. She seemed more animal than human.

"Tell me the truth, Lyla!"

"He's dead," she said.

"How do you know?"

Her chest swelled with the need to say what had been festering in her for months. She would never get over Pat's betrayal, and her mother's blind naiveté and faith in him enraged her.

She stepped forward. Her hand moved to the tie at the back of her neck. She tugged on the string and let the high neck top of her dress fall. It took Beatrice several seconds to register what she'd done. Lyla waited until her eye dropped to the eight stab wounds and three slashes over six inches in length that decorated her chest. They were nothing compared to her mother's scars, but they had clearly been inflicted to kill. A flicker of some emotion wiped the loathing from her mother's face.

"You think I know nothing of pain and suffering?" Lyla whispered. "I know more than you think I do. I've been stabbed, raped, and hunted. I begged for death too, and I didn't get it."

The darkness in her began to spread, roused by her mother's hatred and broken belief in a monster.

"I know what it feels like to watch someone you love be tortured to death. I watched them smash Manny's face in. I listened to him drown in his own blood. I know what it feels like to be utterly helpless. Three years later, I still have nightmares about it every other week."

She traced one of her scars with a shaking finger.

"The man who killed Manny, the man who laughed while he stabbed me, your husband had made a deal with him." She couldn't stop her lips from peeling back in a snarl. Her breathing was harsh and ragged as bloodlust raced through her. "Pat sold Nora and me to him for five hundred thousand dollars. That monster had you raped for insurance. I caught Pat standing over Nora and Carmen with a gun."

She got in her mother's face, blood boiling with the need for violence. She allowed her mother to see the savage she kept under lock and key and was satisfied when Beatrice recoiled.

"What do you think I did, *Mother*?"

Blade's arm pressed against her upper chest, ready to force her back if need be. He knew her control was tenuous at best, that she had lost what patience she had and was going in for the kill.

"I did what any *real* mother would do," she hissed. "I protected my daughter."

Her statement filled the room, which was so quiet she heard the distant murmur of the guards standing in the living room. She waited for Beatrice to make a move, but she was stock-still once more.

"He sent men to kill Nora if Pat couldn't do it. I killed them too." Her voice shook with rage. "You have no idea the sacrifices I've made, the *hell* I've been through. You never came to see me in the hospital. You didn't care that I was fighting for my life. It was all over the news. I disappeared for years at a time, and you never asked why. All you cared about was *him*."

The last word was said on a roar. Blade forced her back a step, and she let him because she was so close to leaping on Beatrice. Years of bitterness choked her.

"Where the *fuck* were you?" Her voice was guttural with rage. "You dare tell me I never helped? I got a job at sixteen to help pay the bills. You gave me to the Pyres because you wanted a fucking dowry for me. All you ever cared about is what you could get out of me. I risked my life to find you, to get to you in time."

Tears spilled down her cheeks. Her nails dug into Blade's arm as she tried to control herself.

"Whether you like it to not, you're my only living parent. Even as useless as you are in that role, you're all I have. The only reason I'm still here is because of Carmen. She lost Vinny, and my death would have pushed her over the edge. She wouldn't let me die, so I fought for her. Since you don't give a shit about anyone but yourself, I suggest you find inspiration because I'm not through with you. I don't care if I have to find someone to spoon-feed you or force you out of bed with a cattle prod. You're not done until I fucking say you're done. You understand me?"

Lyla pulled her top up and turned away as she tied a knot with trembling fingers. She walked out of the house with furious tears streaming down her face. She didn't bother to hide them because she didn't give a fuck. Blade opened the door to the SUV, and she climbed in. The discomfort from her bruised ass was nothing compared to the maelstrom going on inside her.

The short ride back to Aunt Isabel's didn't give her enough time to compose herself. She was still leaking when Aunt Isabel came outside with Nora. Her smile dropped away when she saw Lyla's face.

"Aw, honey, I'm sorry."

"Not your fault. Thank you for watching her and taking Beau and Honey," she said shakily as she took Nora. She strapped Nora in the car seat, grateful for any task to keep her from losing her shit.

Aunt Isabel gave her a hug. "I love you."

She nodded. "Love you too. Thank you."

"Anytime. Enjoy your trip."

"Yours as well."

She climbed in beside the car seat and placed her hand

on Nora's lap. Her daughter lifted her hand and gnawed on her fingers. She stared straight ahead as tears slipped down her cheeks.

Blade turned in his seat to look at her. "Lyla?"

"Take me home," she whispered.

They pulled out of the drive.

"Mum mum," Nora said.

It should have been a beautiful moment—the first time Nora said her name—but all she could think about was her own broken mother. She buried her face in Nora's lap and cried.

When they reached the fortress, she was dry-eyed. Nora must have had a blast at Aunt Isabel's because she was sleeping. Blade put Nora on his shoulder while she walked into the house. She headed for the gym and was trying to tape up her hands when Blade entered.

"Where's Nora?" she asked.

"Living room. We'll hear her if she wakes."

He took over binding her hands. She splayed her fingers, and they both saw how badly she was shaking. He closed his hand around hers.

"Lyla."

She pulled away. "No." She turned her back on him and tipped her head up as if that would hold back the stupid tears. "She needed to know what a monster he is."

He made no comment.

"Even if she told someone I murdered him, she has no proof, right?" When he didn't answer, she turned to face him. "Right?"

"She won't talk," he said.

"How do you know?"

He shrugged.

"Find me someone who's going to ride her ass," she muttered. "She doesn't get to die until I order it."

Blade's grin stopped her in her tracks.

"Why the fuck are you smiling?"

He shook his head. "You've come a long way."

She glared at him. "And you think that's funny?"

"Yes."

"Screw you, Blade."

"You told her the truth she needed to hear."

The screaming tension in her shoulders eased.

"You've given her time. She still has a long way to go, but she wouldn't go any further without what you said today."

"She could just dig in her heels to be a bitch and die to make me feel worse."

"I'll make sure she has the right staff to keep her on her toes."

"Thank you." She paced, the maxi dress floating around her legs as she walked over the gym mats.

"You still want to box?"

She considered and then shook her head. The fact that he supported her decision to tell the truth lifted the weight off her shoulders. Most people would say she needed to be more sympathetic and understanding of her mother, but things weren't getting better. It was time to get real.

She walked toward Blade. He stiffened, but didn't back away. She collided against him and buried her face against his broad chest.

"Thank you."

His opinion meant a lot to her. The fact that he witnessed what happened between her mother and stood between them so she didn't do something she'd regret later said a lot about him. To some degree, he protected her and Gavin from themselves.

"What the fuck?"

She looked around Blade and saw Gavin standing in the doorway.

She glared at Blade. "You didn't."

He didn't have to answer because of course he did.

"I forgive you," she said and patted his chest.

"Didn't ask for forgiveness," he retorted.

She walked to Gavin, and said, "Hold me."

He wrapped his massive arms around her and pulled her tight against him. She rested her cheek against his bulging pec, and muttered, "You know, you'd be more comfortable if you weren't so muscular."

Blade snickered as he passed.

"Do you need another spanking?" Gavin asked.

She let out a shaky sigh. "Maybe some other time."

He rubbed her bare back. "You okay?"

"I will be."

7

BEFORE LYLA OPENED HER EYES, HER LIPS WERE CURVED INTO a smile. The faintest hint of light seeped through the wooden louvers that covered the windows, and she was pinned beneath Gavin's heavy arm. He was deeply asleep, his features completely relaxed. When she slid out of bed, he didn't stir. She tiptoed into the connecting room to check on Nora, who was also dead to the world.

She dressed quietly before she left the master suite and entered the living area. The private villa they rented mimicked a monstrous version of the straw huts the natives had once lived in, but with modern updates that included over five thousand square feet of living space, three pools, and air conditioning. The villa had an incredible layout with lots of indoor-outdoor living space that beckoned them outside to take in the priceless view.

Blade stood on the main terrace, legs braced apart and hands clasped behind his back. He had finally given in to the tropics and changed from slacks to shorts and a black shirt. Despite being over four thousand miles from Las Vegas, he still wore his shoulder holster.

She came up beside him and took in the view. The main terrace faced their private beach, a U-shaped alcove covered in palm trees and tropical plants. Aqua waters stretched out as far as the eye could see. Bora Bora was paradise, pure and simple. The moment she stepped foot on this island, she felt as if she'd arrived on an alternate universe where nothing bad could happen. The air smelled of flowers, the staff was all smiles, and she felt safer than she had in years. It took less than a day for her heartache and anxiety to melt away in the face of such raw, natural beauty.

"Have you ever seen anything like it?" she whispered.

"No," Blade said, his voice just as quiet, almost reverent.

The island had yet to stir. Bora Bora had a drugging effect on all of them. She hadn't slept so peacefully in months. She and Gavin spent the first day napping on the terrace, eating, and listening to the sound of the ocean.

"You like your room?" she teased.

Blade had a minor fit when he found out he was occupying the other suite, which had enough room for four people and its own private pool and hot tub. Gavin rented another villa for the ten guards they brought with them who took shifts patrolling the grounds.

"It's too big," Blade growled.

"It's perfect."

He rolled his shoulders. "It's unnecessary."

She bumped her shoulder with his. "You should take advantage while we're here. Relax, take some time to recoup."

"From what?"

She stared at him. "You're not serious, are you?"

He scanned the beach. "You up for a run?"

She blinked. "Didn't you hear what I just said?"

"You haven't worked out in five days."

She put her hands on her hips. "I'm on vacation! *And* I've been swimming, which burns calories."

"A run won't kill you."

She glared at him for a moment before she let out a disgusted sound. No, a run wouldn't kill her, and the view would be amazing, so if a run would shut him up, fine. She was sitting on the bed putting on her shoes when Gavin spoke.

"What time is it?"

She gave him a quick kiss. "It's still early. Blade and I are going for a run. Nora's still asleep. Watch her for me, will you?"

He grunted and dragged her down for a deeper kiss before he released her.

"What are you smiling for?" Blade asked when she joined him.

"Gavin's sleeping."

"So?"

"He needs it." His baffled expression told her he genuinely didn't understand what she was saying. "Never mind. Let's go."

He had changed into shoes and nixed the guns. Wise, since he wasn't supposed to have them anyway. They strolled quietly beneath the palm trees before they reached the main path, which was some distance from their villa. They started off at an easy jog, a slow enough pace for her to take in the resort. The path wove through a lush wonderland of scents, color, and stunning scenery. Once they reached the beach, her stamina tanked. She had never jogged in sand, so within a half mile, she was gasping for air. Sand churned beneath her shoes, which made her work three times harder than if she were on a firm, flat surface.

"Okay, I'm done," she panted and slowed to a walk.

Blade stopped and turned to her. His shirt was damp with perspiration, but his breathing was still even despite the exertion.

"How are you okay with this?" she asked and kicked the fine white powder.

"I train constantly."

She trained too, but apparently, not as much as him. No matter how hard she worked, she would never get close to keeping up with Blade or Gavin. She mumbled under her breath as they continued along the beach. As she got her breath back, she began to appreciate her surroundings once more. The mint green waters beckoned to her. Gavin hid the one-piece bathing suit she brought and insisted she buy another one. Even though they had a private beach, she wasn't about to parade around in a bikini, but he wouldn't budge. She'd given in to his autocratic demand because the water was every shade of blue imaginable, and she couldn't resist. Inspired by their surroundings, she chose two swimsuits—a cobalt and white bikini. She wasn't happy about her body, but here, she didn't feel as self-conscious. When she wore the bikini yesterday, Blade hadn't batted an eye. She was exasperated that Gavin wouldn't allow her to wear the cover-up or matching sarong. He was such a damn bully. On the other hand, Gavin was embracing their time here, so because of that, she didn't bitch too much.

As they circled back to the villa, she paused at the tip of the island. Even though he'd been a few paces ahead, Blade stopped immediately, attuned to her every move. She closed her eyes and took a deep breath as the breeze tugged on her wayward strands of hair. The urge to toss her arms wide like Rose from the *Titanic* made her smile, but she didn't want to freak Blade out so early in the morning. She rested her hand over her heart and listened to the rhythmic thumping in her ears. She was still here.

"Never imagined I'd see a place like this."

She glanced at Blade who had his shirt draped over one shoulder. He scanned his surroundings before he shook his head.

"I can't take this place in."

She beamed. "Isn't it great?"

"It's something, that's for sure."

His grudging admiration made her smile. Manny had been right. They all needed this—a break from their lives and the violence, deception, and uncertainty that came with it.

As she looked at Blade, her gaze dropped to what looked like old burns on his side. She recognized knife wounds and others scars she couldn't identify. She took a step back and examined five small circles peppered over his shoulder blades. Without thinking, she reached out and touched. He stiffened but didn't pull away. Five shots.

"Is this where ...?"

"Cowards ambushed us and got me in the back."

His back was more scarred than his front. In all the years she'd known him, she'd never seen him without his shirt. He had been concealing his past, just as she was. His body was well sculpted but had been maimed more than Gavin's. She counted fifteen bullet wounds scattered over his body. She traced a deep scar at the top of his spine. A shiver ran down her spine, knowing that a knife had made that cut. She walked around him, examining the layers of scars until she was face to face with him. Her eyes lingered on the tiny slash through his left eyebrow and a recently healed cut, which created a groove in his cheek. Hair thin lines criss-crossed over his chest.

"Why do you do it?" she asked.

Unreadable black eyes held hers for a long minute before he said, "I didn't have a choice. I was born into it."

"Do ... do you want to do something else?"

"No."

No hesitation in his voice. She didn't understand. "Why not?"

"I'm a soldier."

"Is that what you want?"

"It's what I am."

"You can have a life outside the underworld."

"No, I can't."

"Do you have a contract with Gavin?"

"No."

"Then why not try for something different?"

"And leave you?"

She stopped breathing. She wanted what was best for him, but if that meant leaving her ...

His mouth curved before he forced it straight again. He looked beyond her to the ocean. "Once a soldier, always a soldier. We die in combat. That's an honorable death."

"Did you go into the military?"

"You need to graduate from high school to join."

"You didn't graduate?"

"No, I dropped out in the fifth grade."

He could have fooled her. Blade was precise in his actions and speech. He didn't sound uneducated, and he was as rigid as a marine. He was a proud man, much like Gavin. Steadfast, loyal, and ready to put his life on the line. She didn't understand, but she respected it. She owed him her life, yet he asked for nothing and got irritated when she tried to give him things.

"What do you want, Blade?"

Black eyes refocused on her. "I have everything I need."

"But what else do you want? When's your birthday?"

He scowled. "I told you, I don't want anything."

"You're not going to tell me your birthday?"

"It's not important."

She jabbed him in his chest. "Tell me."

He glared at her. "December."

"December what?"

"Twenty-fifth."

She grinned huge. "You're a Christmas baby? That's so *cute!*"

He turned away from her and started back toward the villa.

"That means you have to get at least two presents on Christmas, one for your birthday and one for the holiday," she said as she paced alongside him.

"I don't need anything."

"Oh, stop being such a baby. You must need socks, more black shirts, or ties, right? Oh, I can get you a nice suit."

"I can buy it myself."

"Well, of course you can, but it's better when somebody gives it. Wait!" She grabbed his hand and yanked him to a stop. "What's your real name?"

His eyes narrowed. "I go by Blade."

"I know, but that's a nickname, right?" When he didn't answer, she squeezed his hand. "What's wrong with your real name?"

"I don't like it."

"A lot of people don't like their names but—"

"I was named after someone I hate. I don't use it."

His voice was so agitated that she patted his chest the way she did to placate Gavin. "Okay, Blade it is." She began to walk again and tugged on his hand when he didn't move. "Come on, I'm hungry."

She released him once he started moving again. She spotted the villa in the distance and jumped when their personal security appeared out of nowhere. They acknowledged her with curt nods before they got back to work.

"I don't know why you want to stay with us," she said quietly, without looking at him. "But I'm happy you do."

They were approaching the main terrace when he said, "I have more today than I ever thought I would. I'm not going anywhere."

She grasped his calloused, scarred hand in hers once more and squeezed before she released him. When they walked onto the terrace, they found Gavin sitting at the outdoor dining area with a large fan swirling lazily above him. The table was laden with food, and Nora was sitting in a high chair, dressed in a jewel toned swimsuit.

"Good run?" Gavin asked as he got off the phone.

"Yes." She came up behind him and pressed her cheek to his. "Thank you for this."

"Then give me a fucking kiss."

She grinned as she gave him chaste peck on the corner of his mouth. He grabbed a fistful of her sweaty shirt and forced her to his side so he could pull her down for a real kiss. When he finished getting his taste, he put her in the chair beside him and piled her plate with food.

Blade sat near Nora and took over the feeding Gavin had abandoned. She sat sideways on her chair and leaned into Gavin. "This is the best place on earth."

Gavin grunted and put her plate in front of her. "I might have to steal this chef."

"He is amazing," she said as she cut her crepe. "You slept well?"

He ran a hand down his face. "I slept ten hours and feel like I could sleep ten more."

"You should! We're here for the month. No rush on anything. Sleep is good for you."

They were so used to rushing around and not getting enough sleep, but the quiet, lack of an agenda, and warm humidity made them naturally drowsy. Years of going on so little rest was catching up to him. In the two days they had been here, she had never seen him so relaxed.

"What are you going to do today?" Gavin asked.

"I'm going to swim, eat, nap, and that's about it," she said.

He yawned and nuzzled her as she ate. "Sounds like a full day."

Four hours later, she waded into the lagoon after putting Nora down for a nap. The only sound was that of the birds calling to one another and the gentle lap of water. She could almost imagine that she was on her own private island. Fish wove around her ankles and darted away, scales flashing in the sunlight. Her toes curled in soft sand as her hands swished through the water. She stood waist deep in the enchanting mint green water and took a deep breath before she dived.

She sliced through the water, arms and legs moving in unison. Her lungs burned as she kicked toward the surface. She splashed the water and laughed out of sheer joy. The beauty of this place healed something broken and tarnished inside her, and her heart felt full. She floated on the water, which was still as a lake, and stared up at the sky, which seemed a more vibrant shade than the one back home.

"Lyla!"

She raised her head and looked toward the shore. The staff had set up a table, chairs, and an umbrella in the water. Blade and Gavin were already seated. She swam up to them and easily slipped into her seat and couldn't stop smiling.

"I love it here!"

Gavin's mouth twitched. "You don't say?" he said dryly as he handed her a glass of wine.

She sipped. "Everything tastes better here!"

Blade shook his head and placed his phone on the table, which had a live video of Nora. The staff waded into the water in shorts and trays laden with food. It was bizarre to eat on fine china with gold utensils when she had water lapping around her waist, but she would take it. She noticed some of the server's eyes drift over her scars. She detected sympathy and curiosity, but nothing more. The locals truly accepted them as they were.

Through Gavin, she had been exposed to fine and luxurious experiences, but this was another level. The first course was artfully arranged finger food. These were foods she had tried before, but there was a tropical flair to everything that made the dishes unique and flavorful. Even Blade complimented a steamed shrimp dumpling covered in orange sauce. She didn't realize she cleaned every plate until she caught Blade and Gavin staring at her.

"What?" she asked defensively.

They glanced at each other but didn't answer. When Nora woke from her nap, Blade fetched her. When Lyla tried to take the baby, Nora clung to his chest.

"You should wear a pouch, Blade," she teased.

He gave her a deadpan look as Nora braced her tiny feet on his massive thighs and smacked his bare chest. The servers brought the next course, and Lyla leaned forward eagerly to see the spread. She caught the furtive looks the servers cast between them and wondered about it. As they

walked away, she heard one of them say, "Threesome."
What the ...? She burst out laughing.

"What?" Gavin asked.

She dropped her head back and couldn't stop her hyster-
ical giggles. She, Gavin, and Blade—a polyamorous couple.
Holy smokes. The worst part was, it was a rational conclu-
sion. Blade joined them for what was considered to be a
romantic lunch. Not only that, he had Nora on his lap,
where she was clearly content. If they saw her with him this
morning, it was no wonder they were confused.

"I think she's had too much sun," Blade said.

She took a deep breath to compose herself but snickered
when she saw their bewildered looks. Oh my God, the
thought of Gavin and Blade ...

"Excuse me," she choked and slipped off her seat into
the water.

She dived deep and skimmed the sand with her belly as
she swam. When she came up for air, she was still laughing.
That turned into a shriek when something dragged her
under. She swallowed a mouthful of salt water and came up
gagging and gasping. Gavin appeared in front of her.

She splashed his face. "What the hell!"

She kicked off his belly but didn't get far when he
grabbed her leg and reeled her back in.

"What's so funny?" he asked.

"You nearly drown me to find out why I'm laughing?"

"I wanted to make sure they didn't drug our food, which
would make sense since you ate most of it."

She glared at him. "If you want more food, order it,
killjoy."

He pinned her against him while he waded deeper so
she couldn't touch the bottom.

"Now, what's so funny?" he asked.

"Nothing."

"Lyla."

"You're not going to like it." He eyed her expectantly and she groaned. "Gavin, you don't want to know."

"I have a sense of humor."

"No, you don't."

He scowled. "I do."

She rolled her eyes. "Sure."

He pinched her ass, and she yelped.

"Fine!" She wrapped her arms around his neck and glanced back at the shore before she whispered, "They think we're a couple."

"We are a couple."

She glanced pointedly at Blade and then back at him. *"We."*

He still didn't understand. She tried to smother her mirth against his neck and failed miserably. She figured her meaning finally penetrated because his arms flexed around her.

"That's ridiculous."

His tone was dismissive rather than angry, which showed how much he trusted Blade. Gavin could be jealous of her ex, Marcus, or any other male who got close to her but never his second in command. Blade's loyalty was absolute.

She cupped Gavin's face. "If only they knew what a possessive psycho you are."

He'd left his shades behind, so his hazel eyes were bare. The reflection of light off the water made them appear otherworldly.

"Maybe we should show them how exclusive we are," he said as he ran his finger along the bikini top.

She felt a trill of alarm. "What are you talking about?"

"If they see me fuck you while Blade watches and takes care of the baby, it'll make his position clear."

She jerked. "You wouldn't."

He lifted her and forced her legs around him.

"Gavin."

"What?" he asked lazily as his finger slipped beneath the thin ties of her top.

"We are *not* having sex in front of anyone, least of all Blade!"

"Why not?"

She gawked at him. "You can't be serious!"

"I told you once that I'd fuck you in front of an audience so they could see the way you respond to me. I'd come inside you and let them watch as my cum dripped out of you." He tugged the tie on the back of her top. "There'd be no mistaking who you belong to."

She pressed her chest against his as her top came loose. "Gavin, don't you fucking dare!"

He grinned devilishly. "Convince me."

"What?" He tugged on the strings while she grappled to keep them. "I'm going to kill you!"

"What will you do to make me stop?"

"Anything," she said quickly.

He stopped yanking on her top and she shoved away and tread water while she secured it. She rarely showed her chest, and here she was, in a bikini. Of course, he had to take it one step further and threaten to fuck her in front of people. His gall knew no bounds.

"I'll collect later," he said with a satisfied smile.

"Jerk," she retorted as she swam toward shore.

Blade handed Nora to her when she took a seat to finish eating. Nora was fascinated by the water and kept trying to dive into it. Gavin swam out of the alcove to explore and returned when she and Blade were finished with their meal. She gave him a drop-dead glare which made him laugh as she left the table and finally waded into the water to Nora's delight.

LYLA STOOD on their private terrace just outside their bedroom and watched the sun set. She tried to imprint every color in her mind since her camera couldn't do it justice. Her starving soul drank it in.

Gavin wrapped his arms around her from behind, and she leaned back against him.

"You know how I never ask you for anything?" she murmured.

He settled his chin on her head. "Debatable."

"What have I asked for?" she demanded.

"There's two dogs in my house."

"You love them!"

"Your ex is still breathing."

"You hired him," she muttered.

"And I still allow you to speak to your crazy cousin."

She smacked the massive arms wrapped around her. "You've been saying that since we got together, and you love Carmen."

"She's a bad influence."

"She is a bad influence. That's why she encouraged me to date you." She screeched when he bit her neck.

"That's the one good thing she ever did," he growled.

"And she saved your daughter's life." *And mine,* she thought. "You bitch about her, but you love her like the sister you never had."

He grunted and kissed his bite mark. "What do you want?"

She turned in the circle of his arms. "I want an island," she said bluntly.

He looked beyond her to the sunset. "An island, hmm?"

She tapped his chest nervously. She had never asked Gavin for anything extravagant. She didn't ask for jewelry or designer labels, but the peace she experienced here—that was worth asking for.

His hand smoothed over her bare back as he contemplated the view. She wanted to plead her case but remained quiet instead. She didn't need an answer *now*, but knowing that she could come back anytime, that she had her own haven waiting would make anything she experienced in Las Vegas bearable.

"We'll look tomorrow. There's a bunch of tiny islands all over the place," he said.

Her mouth sagged. "Really?"

"Of course. You think I can't see for myself how happy you are here?"

"But ... you'll really buy me an island?"

"I promised you paradise."

"You meant figuratively."

"I mean it whatever way it needs to be."

She shoved him into the room and knocked him backward on the bed. She covered his face with kisses.

"You are the *best* husband ever!"

She gave him a kiss with tongue. His hand slipped beneath her bikini bottoms. Things were just starting to get dirty when his phone rang.

He tensed. "That's Marcus."

She rolled off him. "You better get it."

He walked out of the bedroom to get his phone while

she danced into the luxurious bathroom and stared at the foolish grin on her face.

"You want to come to my private island?" she asked herself.

She grinned and stripped off her bikini. The massive shower could fit five people. She stepped under copper showerheads and let the waterfall make her squeaky clean. She changed into a flowy nightgown and sat on a lounge chair on the terrace. The only light came from the pool and jacuzzi. She looked up at the stars.

"I can feel things changing," she whispered to Nora who sat between her thighs. "Things are falling into place."

Maybe their luck was changing. Nora gave her a serious look and spoke gibberish as she played with the silky material of her nightgown. She kissed Nora's temple and rocked her until the baby slumped against her. When Nora began to drool, she rose and put her in the connecting room and closed the door. She heard the shower running as she leaned against the open doors that led onto the terrace and sent pictures to Carmen and Aunt Isabel.

"What the hell is this?"

8

SHE TURNED AND SAW GAVIN STANDING IN THE DOORWAY leading to the bathroom. He had a half empty pack of birth control pills in his hand. The cloud of contentment she had been floating on evaporated. Oh, fuck.

"How long have you been on these?" he asked.

She licked her lips before she said, "A month."

Her heartbeat thudded in her ears as he stalked toward her. Even as her body tensed for flight, she forced herself to stay where she was. He held the packet between them as his eyes shot daggers at her.

"Where the fuck did you get these?"

Her body tingled with alarm. Just when she thought she'd hit a sweet spot in life, fate had to cut her feet out from under her to let her know life wasn't a fairy tale. It was an existence filled with ups, downs, and explosives.

"Where did you get it?" he shouted.

Nora's muffled cry reached her ears. She immediately tried to step around him, but Gavin gave her a short shove that made her stagger back and blocked her way. When she looked into his eyes, the hairs on the nape of her neck rose.

"Fucking answer me, Lyla."

It was an indication of how far gone he was that he didn't tend to Nora. Normally, one peep was all it took for him to drop everything to soothe his daughter. Right now, his daughter's distress made no impact upon him. He was completely focused on her and not budging an inch.

"We're back to *this*?" he hissed

He tossed the packet on the floor and stomped on them. "Gavin!"

When she leaned down to pick them up, he jerked her upright. A bolt of pain shot through her arm. She dropped her phone, which slid across the floor. He backed her against the wall and slammed his fists into the wooden panels on either side of her head.

Nora's cry escalated into a piercing scream that she was sure carried to the other guests on the resort.

"Gavin, back off."

He put his hand on her throat. When his hand flexed, she felt a spurt of fear.

"You think I'm playing around? I'm not. Answer my fucking question before I beat it out of you. You haven't gone to a doctor. Who gave them to you?"

"I already had the pills. They're the ones the doctor gave me after we married," she snapped and yanked at his wrist with no results.

"You mean the ones you asked for?" he asked softly.

She glared at him. "Yes."

The door opened. She couldn't see beyond Gavin's bulk, but there was only one person who dared to enter.

"What the fuck, Gavin?" Blade asked.

"Get her out of here," Gavin ordered and then smothered her with his body. "Nora, not Lyla."

She heard the soft tread of Blade's footsteps as he

crossed the room. Nora's wails got louder when he opened
the door. Blade's gravelly voice softened as much as it could
as he comforted her. Gavin didn't move an inch as Blade
came back into their suite. Out of the corner of her eye, she
saw Blade standing several feet away with Nora in his arms.
Her baby reached for her, for once not placated by Blade.
Once more, she tried to move, but she was completely
immobilized and the grip on her throat kept her from
talking to Blade or reassuring Nora.

Her eyes pricked with tears as she glared at Gavin. The
vacation was over. Three days of good and then she came
crashing back to reality. He went from loving husband to
merciless ass so easily. The brutal rage in the hazel depths
promised her that she would be punished for lying to him.

"Get the fuck out," Gavin snarled.

"Gavin—"

"Out, Blade!"

"Don't make me fucking kill you," Blade said in a
menacing voice she had never heard from him before.

Blade slammed the door so hard it shuddered in its
frame. Gavin rested his lips against her temple in a mockery
of affection as the hand against her throat trembled.

"Every time I think we're on the same page, every time I
think I have you where I want you, you do something that
makes me feel unsure of you *again*." His tone was soft,
almost gentle, which made his words all the more chilling.
"I've fought long and hard for you. Now, tell me why you're
guarding your body against having more kids with me and
don't you fucking lie to me."

His hold loosened so she could get take a full breath.
She'd known if he discovered the pills, he'd be angry, but
she hadn't expected him to go on a rampage. If they had
been home, Blade would have sedated and locked him in

the basement. Instead, she was going to have to face the monster with no backup.

As if he could read her thoughts, he said, "No one's going to save you. Now, talk."

"You won't understand," she said hoarsely.

"I know I won't understand! How could you do this to me? How could you lie to me?"

"I'm not ready."

"I fulfilled my end of the deal. You told me you'd stay with me if I gave up being crime lord. Now, you give me what I want."

"We have Nora."

"I want more kids. I said so right from the start. I asked you less than a week ago if you took a pregnancy test. I've never hidden the fact that I want more. Why the fuck are you holding back on me?"

When she didn't respond fast enough, he gripped her chin and lifted it. They glared at one another. He leaned down so she could see the beast watching her.

"You make me feel more than any other person on the planet. You should take care that you don't push me too far," he warned.

"Don't threaten me," she hissed.

"You don't know how close I am to putting my hands on you."

She raised her chin. "You already have."

"Tell me why, Lyla."

"It's my body," she whispered.

"Is that what this is about? Your body?" Before she could answer, he muttered, "That's not it."

"It *is* my body!"

"You carried Nora well, and you know I don't care about the stretch marks or scars. That's life."

"The scars are part of our lives, not everyone else's."

"What does that mean?" When she didn't answer, he shook her. "Talk to me, damn it!"

Her husband hadn't grown up in the same world she had. He was born to fight and kill for what he wanted. She fell into a gray category he didn't know how to deal with. She would never be sure that he could control himself when his emotions were roused.

"You want to know why?" she asked.

"Yes," he said through clenched teeth.

"Then let me go."

His large chest expanded to capacity. She expected him to roar or go for her throat again. She could see him fighting with himself. She waited, knowing the scales could tip either way. When he ripped himself from her and walked away, she slumped against the wall. She watched the muscles in his back shift with detached fascination as he tried to control himself.

She ran her hand over her tender throat. She knew he wouldn't understand, which is why she hadn't discussed it with him. She did what was best for her.

Knowing she had a limited time to state her case made her anxiety rise. A warm breeze drifted over the cold sweat on her skin. Fragmented thoughts sped through her mind. Her heart began to race, and her body went numb from a chill that came from her soul. She could feel the panic attack coming along with the memories that wanted to drag her under. She braced her hands on her knees as she tried to catch her breath. She could still feel the impact of the shield as it connected with pliant flesh; the sound of snapping bone sounded sharp and delightful in her ears ... She shook herself and tried to banish the sound of the crowd in the pit as they cheered her on.

"Lyla."

She blinked several times before she was able to focus on Gavin who stood several feet away.

"I would do anything for you," he said in a voice that gave away his thirst for violence. "And I expect the same in return."

"I can't get pregnant again because I'm not okay, Gavin, and neither are you."

"We were fine until I found out you were lying to me."

She straightened, arms crossed over her chest, as she whispered, "You weren't there."

"I wasn't where?"

"You weren't there when I found my dad standing over Nora and Carmen."

"What?"

She paced in front of the open doors that led onto the terrace. She could feel his impatience from across the room and knew she was running out of time. She tried to assemble her words so she could make him understand.

"That night, it was me against them. *Eight* of them. No backup, no idea what I was doing." She shuddered as an acrid taste filled her mouth. "I found Pat standing over them with a gun. He's always been a shit, but I never thought he could ... How could he? If I had opened the door two seconds later, if I had stayed outside, I would've lost them." The thought chilled her to the core. "They *hunted* Nora. If I hadn't killed those men, if Blade hadn't come in time, if I hadn't had another gun to give Carmen ..." She could barely breathe past the terror. "We almost fucking lost her!"

"But we didn't."

"But we were so close to—"

"Vega and your fucking father are *dead,* so what the fuck are you talking about?"

"They're dead, but other people like them are still out there!" she shouted. "Nora's had a bounty on her head before she was born, and you want to bring more kids into that? I can't protect her, and neither can you! When it came down to it, I had to hand her off to Carmen and tell her to run. I watched Manny die. I saw what they did to my mom. Do you know what they could do to a child?" The horror of such a thing made her lightheaded with terror. "Having more children is more ammunition against us, more ways to manipulate and exploit us. I can't lose a child, Gavin. I wouldn't survive—"

"You won't."

His quick, sure answer enraged her.

"How can you promise me that? Look at my mother! Everyone around us pays a price. Being in this life has taken a toll on me. I have waking nightmares, panic attacks, and my mood swings are insane. I hallucinate. I thought I saw Steven in the nursery one day, and I almost fired my gun. I could have hurt Nora; I could have hurt myself!" She hugged herself tight to stop herself from falling apart as she paced restlessly. "There are days, sometimes even weeks where I think I'm good, that I'm past it, but it always comes back." She glared at him as a tear slipped down her cheek. "You think four months is long enough to move on? That I should be cured and ready to pop out more babies by now? I'm not. I'm not okay. And I don't know if I ever will be."

She swiped at her streaming eyes. She'd said her truth, and from the looks of it, he still didn't get it. Well, how could he understand? He believed he was invincible. She knew for a fact that she wasn't. That night at the safe house, she had done everything that was required of her, yet in the end, Nora's life had been in Carmen's hands. If Carmen hadn't pulled the trigger ...

"After my first kill in the pit, I couldn't sleep for days."

She stopped in her tracks and looked at him. His hands were clasped behind him, back ramrod straight. He didn't continue; he just watched her with an intensity that made her want to back away.

"How old were you?" she asked.

"Twelve."

Her stomach dipped. "Manny put you in the pit at *twelve*?" His words from the dream came back to her. *I'm a bad man, baby girl.* What the fuck, Manny?

"It was good training," he said, voice devoid of emotion. "I started falling asleep in school. When I came home, Dad had me beaten to toughen me up."

A chill traveled up her spine. She couldn't align Manny with the monster Gavin was describing.

"Dad kept putting me in the pit. I had nightmares for years, but I got past it. I had the same stuff you do now—panic attacks, hallucinations, and fear."

He walked toward her, and she took a step back. His jaw clenched, but he didn't stop until he was directly in front of her.

"Am I a bad man?"

She jerked. "What?"

His eyes bored into hers. "Am I a bad man?"

"You can be," she said.

"To you? Am I a bad man?"

"Sometimes."

"And the other times?" he asked with an edge to his voice.

"You're a dream."

He reached out slowly and cupped her cheek. His thumb stroked her skin as he said, "I didn't grow up in a loving home. I didn't grow up with a mom or siblings. I went to school during the day, and when I came home, I was trained to kill. I put my life on the line once a month. Every time I stepped into the pit, I had to know I was gonna win. It's all in your head. If you're the best, then you are."

She understood what he was saying in his Gavin way but, "I'm not the best."

"You're stronger than you think you are. You think you're broken, but you're not." His hold on her firmed. "You will get better."

She gripped his wrist. "I believe that, but I still want time."

His eyes hardened. "I'm not going to let you hold us back."

"We aren't being held back. We're living life and enjoying it."

"You want Nora to have backup? She needs siblings. They'll protect each other. Family is everything."

"But it's not over."

"It is," he ground out. "Vega's dead."

"What about Lucifer?"

His eyes narrowed. "Don't worry about Lucifer. I'll handle him."

Lucifer saved her life, yet he was also the catalyst behind Steven's deranged plan. She couldn't wrap her mind around Lucifer's motives. He was, in turns, abhorrent, logical, childish, and insane.

"Why would he double-cross Steven to make a deal to visit us once a year? It doesn't make sense."

This talk was long overdue. They hadn't discussed what happened in Hell, and she'd been happy to ignore it, but it was time to bring it out in the open.

"Blade convinced him that you're unique."

She blinked. "Unique, how?"

"Lucifer's fascinated by those in the real world who have his ... tendencies."

"What tendencies?"

"Mayhem, violence, murder."

"He thinks I'm like *him*?"

"And you're mine," he added.

"So?"

"Lucifer's known me a long time. I've never cared for anything the way I care for you. I would have bartered anything to get you back, and that intrigued him."

"Lucifer mentioned you're the closest thing he has to a brother," she said quietly.

"We were the youngest to ever be put in the pit and survive. That's all we have in common." He pressed his forehead against hers. "I didn't want kids. I wasn't going to get married. I didn't want any vulnerabilities ... and then I met you."

She pressed her hand against his chest. "Don't."

He placed his hand over hers. "You made me want things I shouldn't. I should have let you live a normal life. I didn't. I should have let you live on the road with Carmen. I didn't. I should have given you time before getting you pregnant. I didn't. I should have been at the safe house to save you from having to do what you did. I've made you break every moral you have. I'll ask for more because we don't live in a world where we can afford to have the same code as everyone else."

He pushed her down on the bed and hovered over her with one hand on her stomach.

"There's nothing more that I want in this world than to have more children."

She swallowed, unsure if she could give him that.

"We owe it to Vinny and my dad to live life to the fullest.

Nora's my redemption, but the others will make it that much sweeter. Nora needs other to take the heat too because we're gonna try to control everything, and she needs them to commiserate with. You're lucky enough to have Carmen. I had Vinny. What would life have been like without them?"

Her heart ached. Carmen was everything to her. She wouldn't be alive today without her. "Stop."

"We can do this. I won't let you down."

"It's not about that. It's—"

He lifted her nightgown.

"It's about ..." She was distracted when he licked her belly button. "You never know what's going to happen in future and—cut it out!"

He grabbed her leg and bent it up. "I know what's going to happen. You're going to get better and give me what I want."

"In time, I ..." she hissed when he began to lick her.

"I love you more than I thought I could. I want everything you have to give. No half measures, no waiting. The kids will be prepared. We'll make sure of it. Don't worry about Lucifer." He breathed against her clit. "He won't be an issue."

"You don't know that. You ..." Her eyes rolled to the back of her head.

"I know I love you. Nothing will change that. I want babies with you. I want you pregnant. It'll be a big fuck you to everyone who thinks we should be scared. You want them to think we're afraid, baby?"

"No, I ... I don't know."

"I told you when I wanted Nora that we were going to move on with our lives, and I'm telling you the same thing now. You don't stop nature from taking its course, and you don't keep secrets from me."

He bit her inner thigh, and she kicked him in the shoulder with her other foot. He rose and slid into her.

"You're going to give me what I want," he decreed. "You don't get time because I don't know how much we have. If I died tomorrow, I want to know that tonight I got you pregnant, you understand?"

It finally clicked. If she lost him, that is exactly what she wanted. She wanted another piece of him. Nora wouldn't be enough.

"You'll give me warriors," he announced as he shoved himself deep. "Our kids won't grow up the way I did. You'll love them and infuse them with your spirit. They'll be trained to learn how to protect and defend. They can live however they want. That's the legacy you gave them by having me step down from my position, and I'll honor it."

"Gavin."

"I sacrificed everything to have you, and I'm going to get everything I can out of you. I *need*." His head kicked back as he lost himself in her. "Too much. I'll never stop needing."

He began to thrust hard, dragging her to the edge where the mattress was firmer so he could go deeper.

"Take my cum. Take it deep. Fuck yeah."

After he finished filling her, he pulled back and stared at her dripping pussy. He smacked her, and she jumped.

"What the hell!"

"Don't you ever do something like that without talking to me again," he growled as he slipped his hand through his sperm and pushed it back inside her. He rubbed her sensitive clit. He knew exactly what she liked. It didn't take long before she was crying out beneath him. He slipped back into her as she came. His smile was feral as she milked him. He stayed in her until he was hard again and then fucked her until he blew another load.

"I'm calling in my favor."

"What favor?" she mumbled against his skin.

"Today, in the water, you said I can have anything I want."

She sighed. "You always get your way. It's not fair."

"I know what's best for us." He rolled her on top of him and rested his face in the hollow of her neck. "I'm going to give you everything you want, but it's a two-way street. Some of the things I want, you don't think you can give. I'll be the judge of that."

"Arrogant."

He nibbled on her neck. "No, I'm the fucking best."

9

A LOUD KNOCK ROUSED HER FROM A SOUND SLEEP. SHE opened her eyes as Gavin rolled away from her. She sat up as he pulled on his pants. It took her a few seconds to recognize the master suite of the villa cast in moonlight. The warm, tropical breeze ruffled her hair as it drifted through the open terrace doors.

"Gavin?" she murmured.

"Hold on," he said and grabbed his gun before he walked to the door.

When he opened it, she blinked blearily at the figure in the doorway.

"Blade?" she mumbled and glanced at the clock. It was two in the morning. What the hell? She rolled over and dragged the sheets over her head. She had just drifted back to dreamland when someone shook her awake.

"Lyla."

A light came on, and the sheets were tugged away. She groaned and peered at Gavin's face. She was so tired, she felt drunk. As his face swam into view, she registered the hub of activity in the living room and multiple male voices. As her eyes wandered over him, she saw that he had gotten dressed before waking her.

She sat up so fast, she felt lightheaded. "What's wrong? Where's Nora?"

"It's not Nora. She's still asleep," Gavin said quietly.

"What's going on?"

He stared at her for a long moment, conflicting emotions in his golden eyes before he said, "Carmen's missing."

"Carmen?" That was the last thing she expected to hear. She relaxed. "She's probably out partying or something."

"Angel called. They have footage of her being attacked by the Black Vipers."

She stared at him for thirty seconds, unable to comprehend what he was saying. "What?"

"We're waiting for word."

"Word on what?"

He opened his mouth and then closed it. All trace of sleep fell away as his implication hit her like a ton of bricks.

"You're waiting to see if someone will call in a ransom or word on her body?"

He was trying to be calm for her sake, but his energy leaked from his pores. He was worried, and that fucking terrified her. Dread and fear dug its talons into her heart.

"She has bodyguards, doesn't she?"

"Mickey was found dead at the club where she was taken."

It was starting all over again. Her skin burned as a chilling cold swept through her.

"You told me no more," she whispered.

"Lyla, we're going to get her back."

She got on her knees and grabbed two fistfuls of his shirt. "This can't happen again. I can't lose my sister, Gavin. She's ... she's a part of us. If she—"

He cupped her cheek and brushed a kiss over her trembling lips. His voice was a sinister rumble as he promised, "You won't have to. I'm going to find her." He kissed her once more and brushed away her tear. "Get packed. We're going home."

AUTHOR'S NOTE

Hi everyone,

I hope you enjoyed Crime Lord's Paradise. I decided to write Gavin and Lyla's trip to Bora Bora as an extra scene for book 5 and within a day, realized I could expand it into something longer. This novella was a surprise to me and a welcome stress reliever. I've never been with any characters as much as I have with Gavin and Lyla. I fell into them as if I never left. I know where everything is in their house, what they're thinking, and what they want. Freaking weird.

I had a great time writing this. If you follow me, you know I love character development and am always down for digging a little deeper, which is what this novella is about—adjusting the lens so we can see more color and depth in these characters for the future. I love trotting alongside characters and observing. I thought I was the only one who thought this was interesting, but it sounds like a bunch of you are down for the ride!

I have to thank everyone who has been so patient about book 5, even with such a terrible cliff-hanger. Books 5 and 6 have intersecting plots and timelines, which is why it's taking so long. I will be working on both novels during the winter and releasing book 5 (part 2 of Carmen's story) in early 2019.

Thank you all for your support, encouragement, and well wishes. They definitely make a difference and remind me how engaged people are with the stories. Not so long ago, I was writing for my own entertainment. It's crazy that there's a whole community waiting to see what happens next. It's amazing and extremely humbling. I always try to craft the best story I can and that definitely takes time, so please be patient.

If you enjoyed Crime Lord's Paradise, please leave a review! I will post any news I have about future releases as soon as I have any so look out for my newsletter, blogs, or social media (I prefer Instagram and Facebook. Twitter... I have no idea what I'm doing. LOL).

Thank you for your support!

Love,

Mia Knight

BOOKS BY MIA KNIGHT

ABOUT THE AUTHOR

Mia is the author of the Crime Lord Series and writes dark, contemporary romances. She currently lives in Sin City where she is shadowed by her dogs who don't judge when she cries and laughs with the characters in her head. She loves road trips, fast food, lakes and rivers, trains, and daydreaming.

Stalk Mia
Website
Email
Mia Knight's Captives (Facebook Group)

f facebook.com/miaknightbooks

🐦 twitter.com/authormiaknight

📷 instagram.com/authormiaknight

g goodreads.com/authormiaknight

BB bookbub.com/profile/mia-knight